Scale the Sycamore

J. Gray

Table of Contents

Art

Dear Reader,

    Scale the Sycamore began as a pet project. An idea to simply write a short(ish) trilogy quickly blossomed into so much more. What was to follow were numerous stories and even more poems that were eventually sculpted into one overarching piece. The *Day Job* trilogy remains both the foundation and the keystone to the entire body of work. Every story and every poem has been meticulously placed. As such, Dear Reader, you should make sure to keep these three in the forefront of your mind as you turn each page.

    Scale the Sycamore explores life amidst predatory politics, a debauched society, and a devastated environment. How do we act when faced with despair and isolation? What do we do when our hand is forced by external, sometimes malevolent forces? Ultimately, what is our next move as both an individual and as a whole, as a society?

    Amidst these questions, I began to ponder another: what exactly is he asking us, the reader, to do? What is his prescription after all is said and done and all the chips have fallen? I have spent hours mulling over this idea and realized, basically, that it does not matter what he is asking of us. Rather, it is what the words on the page are asking of us. When push comes to shove, authorial intent means shit.

A. Puri
Busan, South Korea
December 2015

"What are these barriers that keep people from reaching anywhere near their real potential? The answer to that can be found in another question and that's this: Which is the most universal human characteristic: fear, or laziness?"

Louis MacKay in "Waking Life"

"You can find meanness in the least of creatures, but when God made man the devil was at his elbow. A creature that can do anything. Make a machine. And a machine to make a machine. And evil that can run itself a thousand years, no need to tend it. You believe that?"

Cormac McCarthy, "Blood Meridian"

"Can't waste a day when the night brings a hearse."

Rage Against the Machine, "Down Rodeo"

Such curious things, these little shapes we call letters. Individually, they mean basically nothing. But a group of them together, in the right order, and you have a word — by itself nothing remarkable — but still a quite impressive little thing. Think about it for a second: humans decided, over thousands of years, that some random loops and lines would not only mean something, but the right configuration of these loops and lines would be a placeholder for unspeakably immense elements of our lives.

Ecstasy. Courage. Fascination. Deceit. Misery. Fear.

When you tie a string of these configurations together, you have this profound tool that is a sentence. This, my friends, this is the beginning of something grand. When each word compliments the other, stands on the proverbial shoulders and hoists the next even higher, then the potency of each syllable grows exponentially.

Once you begin to braid those strings together into a rope, well, then you've got something cosmic. Or, as some used to say, divine.

Letters, I've discovered after seeing the

world swallowed by flames and the sea, are quite like people.

We had a chance to compose the most marvellous of books.

Instead, we crafted our own noose.

I have here the few scraps of what survived. Of what I've found. All of it is from moments just before and during our great unbinding. I don't know if anyone's made anything since.

I sit at the base of a tree, the only healthy one I've seen in years, and the branches look mighty inviting. In my lap is this moldered collection of stories and poems, and I'm curious how they fit together, if they do. If I should add my own curious little shapes to them. Wondering if it would matter.

But the sun is bright, it's warm, and I'm somehow not coughing up blood. I'm going to take a break from sifting through these configurations and loosening the knots in the strings. See what you can make of them.

I think I might just go for a climb.

we sat on our throne with delusions of answers

now our crown is rotten

Grand Pas de Troix

Kevin, standing a paltry six foot four inches with a barrel chest and a handsome face, stepped from the bathroom as the light faded and the toilet flushed itself. He approached the refrigerator and a display on the door turned on showing what food was inside, the date it was put there, a suggested date of disposal, as well as an expandable list of recipes each could be used in. He walked past a row of cabinets, all of which did the same thing, then reached for a cup next to the sink and filled it with filtered water from the tap. He looked at the kitchen table and after a moment a hologram of three female dancers appeared on the table. He sighed at the delay and rubbed his freshly shaved face. His skin was clear and taut, absent of wrinkles. *Watch Me Now*, in its sixteenth or seventeenth season, promised a huge surprise last night and Kevin couldn't afford to be left out of the loop. He mixed up two of the judges' names while talking about the show at work last week and people were still making jokes. After pouring out half the glass he picked up the hologram with a two handed gesture and tossed it in between two couches in the next room, but the gesture wasn't perfect and the hologram twisted and scaled so large that one of the dancer's feet filled both rooms, pumping up and down to a low-volume melody.

"This piece of," he muttered to himself as he carefully adjusted the image. The trio of women, slightly larger than life, swung arms and twisted hips in the middle of the room. Kevin flopped onto the couch to peer up their skirts. When he landed his chest jiggled a bit, as if he had a water balloon under his shirt. He peered under his collar and frowned at the acne on his chest that was taking so long to fade. His pecs and stomach were slightly swollen as well. "I'm twenty-fuck-ing-six," he said to himself, "a grown ass man, and why, why the shit," he said, shaking his head and popping a few pimples. He sighed and put his shirt down, turning up the volume of the music with another gesture.

He'd seen these dancers once or twice before and so was bored with them quickly. He looked around his apartment, a pouty turn to his lips, when something on the side of the refrigerator caught his eye. He stood up and walked across the room, the girls kept dancing and he was halfway through them when a fourth body joined the choreographed fray. Kevin smiled when he saw it was the president. So this was the big surprise. A little overhyped, but at least he saw it. The camera panned out as the trio formed a semicircle around the commander-in-chief, who dipped into a breakdancing routine just as a banner unfurled, reminding the audience that this was her state of the union address. The camera zoomed out so much the president and her dancers were knee high with the State banner dwarfing them. Kevin chuckled and thought about what he'd say to Tyree and Sam at work tomorrow, when he saw it on the carpet.

Fury washed over him as he brought his eye to the quarter-sized stain. Red wine. It was already set. "They're new, they're new," he repeated, arms and neck bulging. "They won't miss it next time," his hands flexing. He started taking long, slow breaths, his large chest expanding and releasing air in regular intervals, just like Dr. Ilarius told him. He cracked his neck and remembered the note, got up and walked to the refrigerator, unfolded it, saw all the words and sighed.

The first line of the note, "If you care about your future, please read the following with great care." was printed below a logo of two palms cupping a radiant light. The paper was crisp and manila, the ink a perfect black. Before paging his wife in the soundproof entertainment room and reading the note with her in growing shock, Kevin Ballmer flipped the paper over, saw nothing, then glanced out the window at the distant fire raging in the valley, thankful now for the fire insurance he bought from the consultants who visited a few weeks ago. He filled the glass in the sink again and took a long sip before dumping the rest and walking into the lounge room and sitting down. The chair was a gift from their neighbor, Takei Mitsusoko, who lived a few kilometers away. With one hand he closed the President's routine, then ordered the house to page his wife.

Jean Ballmer walked through the wide expanse of the kitchen, rubbing her eyes and wobbling a bit, complaining about their six month old Virtual Cinema Emulator and how it didn't have the scent generation system of the newest version. Cashmere shorts hugged her shapely hips, the matching top had an elaborate tiger stitched into it, the cat's ears bulging with her large but firm breasts. Her legs were long, toned, and free of any blemish.

She sat next to Kevin and leaned into him with a kiss on the head. "What's that?" she asked, her eyes adjusting to the two dimensional paper.

He sighed. "I'm . . . I'm not really sure. I think it's a bill for something?"

"A bill?" she said, snatching the paper away and reading from the beginning.

If you care about your future, please read the following with great care. In compliance with the Wealth Retention Act, The United Planning Frontier has recently visited your home in the interest of preserving the greatest achievement of our species—material wealth. As lifespans continue to shorten, it is paramount to ensure that your family maintains such wonderful comfort and preferred status. By preserving your wealth and family, you contribute to the proliferation of the State—and therefore humanity. Although this task may seem daunting, it is really quite simple: We can achieve continued comfort and status by simply extending qualified family trees.

Yours included.

But what good is a tree without roots? We here at UPF provide the necessary stability for your wealth preservation needs by eliminating the most destabilising element: personal choice.

As UPF takes orders on a quarterly basis, please see below for our contact dates, during which one of our negotiation agents will contact you over the phone to schedule a face to face meeting for a conception consultation.

> *For You, For Us, For the World.*
> *United Planning Frontier.*

*   *   *

Seven year old Jamesie had a cleft palate, six fingers on each hand, an enlarged right eye and a swollen tongue. "If you hears it," he said in a cracked voice to no one in particular, as his family was walking quickly around him. "It's be done. It's be too late. Least that's what's be said at the fountain." He whispered the final word as if it contained a special power, whereby speaking it would release it into the world and wreak havoc. All seven of them, except him, folded and packed in a flurry of arms, tattered blankets and bare feet. Poblano and Jack, his older twins with asthma, bumped into each other. The monocles they used, which used to be glasses, fell on the floor and for half a breath the room paused. They realized the glass wasn't cracked after an agonizing second, and the bustle continued. The family's one window was broken months ago and voices from the street poured through, giving the orange glow of the sky a tremulous soundtrack. When Poblano was in a rush, his club foot usually made Jamsie's insides giggle (even though he could never show it), but not tonight. Nothing would make his insides giggle tonight.

This much he knew.

Gramps stood huge in the center of the room, towering over everyone with his six feet, and watched as the packing was finished and everyone looked at him. He wanted to hug his hunched and wheezing wife, but didn't want his grandchildren to think of it as a goodbye or a sign of dependence. "It's time to go," he finally said, looking at the door and its rusty hinges, the voices outside growing louder.

"Where?" Reej asked, fourteen with a bulbous forehead and ears that fused to the sides of his head. The syllable was more rasp than word. The family stood and let the word settle in the filthy corners of the room, worm about their minds. They all exchanged glances, their faces smeared with dirt, scars large and small writ across their hands and arms, clothes thick with grime, eyes wet with fear. They were all sweating after the bustle of packing what little they had, their stench familiar but unloved.

"The riverbank?" Cocasoff asked, her voice low and heavy in the small room. "It won't be as crowded, and we can—"

"We don't haved any them chemical masks," Poblano interrupted. "We might be as well marched into them fire itself."

"We can be trade for some," Jack said.

"Be trade *what?*" Poblano held his arms open and looked around the one room. The family had finished packing in about two minutes. The stillness of the orange outside was changing, growing into a wild red dance that flickered on his family's skin.

"We can't be stayed," Gramps said. The voices outside were a bizarre mess of speech and shrieks, distant calls for help and people's names. The runner who'd dashed through a few minutes ago had no hair on half of his body and the fear in his screams made them start packing their things. Jamesie walked to the door and used his better eye to peer out. A few people began pointing decades old cell phones to the sky and shouting what they thought would save them. Some pried the backs off their devices and laid out the innards with great care, sincerely believing this would aid their salvation. The undercurrent of chaos was everywhere, tugging at ankles and hitching in voices. Jamesie shifted his feet and rubbed his hands together, bringing color to his albino knuckles.

The family carried what they could and left their two room prefabricated box that had been allotted to Gramp's dad when the ocean swallowed the land.

They fell in with a hundred or so others who looked identical to them and together they walked into their unknowable future.

Without leaders, decisions were made by mob democracy. A few voted to run, and just like that the stampede was born.

Their collective wheezing ended all speech and most slowed to a trot within minutes, their faces pink and slick, chests heaving. The fire was upon them and chased them through the street, devouring garbage and fallen elderly alike. People dropped their few belongings and ran for what was left of their lives. The stench of the river wafted up from the left, but the narrowing dirt road corralled them closer to each other, the trees on their right were all dead and sharp and dense like unlit matches.

"That fire," little Jamesie said into his grandfather's ear, who was a fair bit ahead of the rest of the family, "be runs really fast. Do you be thinked that fire be helps Mom and Pap? In the faxes they be went to?" The child breathed coarse air and not waiting for an answer watched the inferno approach with incredible fouettés and towering pirouettes that hopped over treetops and roofs, spreading itself everywhere. He never knew anything like this could exist, or how it could even happen, what ignorance or evil or misplaced goodwill could bring such a terrible beauty so quickly and violently into his life, into everyone's. When the box he was born in was inhaled in an instant, all fear left Jamesie and he began to watch the blaze, see it for what it really was. It was simply cosmic hinges guiding a door to shut out their existence. He wondered briefly who'd pushed it from the other side, and why.

The only sound heard above the roar was the collective retching of those closest to the water and the wheezing of those approaching. The mass of bodies hit a bottleneck on the banks of the river, some sprinted to the left and right, gagging, their skin sliced by the thickets while more still pushed into centuries of industrial refuse.

Paul had lost his family and pushed his way towards the growing heat and climbed the thickest tree he could find. Its bark was invaded by rot and he saw a thick rope, far too high for him to grab, also rotten and unusable. He was a meter above the mass of family and friends when a blast of hot air almost knocked him down. He shielded his eyes against the coming hell. He turned and looked across the river, up an ancient mountain that was now a hill and at the lights that shone there. The wall, pitch black against the purple and red sky, stood as it had since he could remember, tall and strong. Those domestic lights were all the stars his people had now, and they served the same purpose as the stars of millennia ago: simple evidence of unknowable worlds and galaxies that somehow existed in the same universe. The masses just beneath his feet cried out, some in unison, others at their own wild pitch, but no one moved. They were stuck. Blocked by their past and engulfed by their present, Paul released his grip and let his weight balance him on the branch, waiting for the inevitable to take hold and lead him to death.

A tiny pale wrist shot into the air and Paul's eyes followed. A massive red tube was floating not a hundred meters above, it had white lights blinking like uncertain comets. Its rotating wings pushed cool air onto his face and it seemed for a moment that the roar of the fire and his people's suffering were blotted out by this metallic angel, but the helicopter floated on across the river and up the hill. If there were groans of despair none were heard, for the screams of the burned began. Paul slumped forward as the thin wrist fell into the crowd. Dredges of the river were kicked up in a frenzy of crossing, but the river was too choked with scrap metal and rotten lumber for anyone to wade all the way across, and those who tried suffocated and died in pain. The flames rushed quickly through the crowd, searing flesh from bone and devouring screams of the dying with its own incomprehensible roar.

*　　*　　*

Captain Kaley Collins snapped her window open as she looped around the residence to double back to the fire, then hovered a few kilometers away from the property, breathing slow and deep through her nose. "Burgers after?"

Her copilot, Adam Gentile, thought for a moment then shrugged and nodded. "You payin?" She smiled in response, chewing a huge wad of nicotine gum, pushing the nose of the helicopter down.

"Can't let it cross the river," she said, closing the window.

"Yeah, it'd eat up these hills in a minute."

"Not that, it's just in the contract." She looked at him.

"You didn't read it?"

"I'm just here to deliver the payload. On target and on time. I like to leave the thinking stuff up to you," Adam smiled at her, his curly red hair and blue eyes covered by his helmet and visor. "Besides, I'm more of a people person." She chuckled and pushed on the throttle.

Beyond the wall of flame was an ocean of embers. Miles beyond that was the liquid ocean. A few years before you could even smell it, but the smoke was thick and full of chemicals. The fire season never ended.

"Let's get in position," Kaley said, nodding at Adam who unbuckled his harness and knelt in front of a viewfinder built into the hull, just behind his seat. From here he could determine the best time to drop their payload. 10,000 liters of fire suppressant that would douse any flame it touched by bursting into a huge glob of foam, suffocating it. What didn't burst into foam stuck for a few days, supposedly to prevent future fires.

"Pull along with a greater lean on the eastern bank. We can put out what's left of it and still get a strong coat on the western side," he instructed. "The rest of it will turn back and burn itself out. Hopefully," he added. Two weeks ago part of the river went up, which the bosses weren't too happy about.

"Roger. Doubling back for effect." Kaley, while in a looping left turn, saw a house a few kilometers away. She wasn't sure if they'd been consulted yet. Fire safety consulting was a booming business. "Approaching target." Adam adjusted the viewfinder and began a mental countdown which reached six before continuing out loud. He put his thumb on a large green button. The helicopter tilted and he pressed down. The bay doors slammed open and their payload raced to the flames. The series of massive *whumps* of the foam expanding put a smile on their faces. It was the sound of getting paid.

"Check the maps for that house over there," Kaley said, pointing the nose of the chopper toward the houser. "See if they're available for a consultation." After Adam sat and strapped himself in he pulled out a tablet and swiped open a map, made a three-fingered gesture above it and a holographic menu popped up that he began scrolling through. "Nope. They're free," he said after a minute of searching.

"Wanna get the gear ready? I'll take her up nice and high for the cinematic entrance." Adam chuckled and walked to the back of the cabin, taking a few minutes to organize what they needed. Kaley began their descent as Adam sat back down. "Wanna trade this time?" She asked and he snorted at the old joke.

"I will if you let me fly back," he said with a grin.

"And put my baby in harm's way? Those nozzles back there must be a bit loose."

Kaley brought the chopper down with great slowness, watching the couple huddling together at their door in each other's arms. She set the engine to shut itself off in thirty minutes. They climbed out the rear cargo door wearing gas masks, large tanks strapped to their backs, small duffle bags in one hand and their other extended, palm first. It always surprised them how nervous a uniform made people, and just how quickly it could calm them. Adam did the talking while Kaley began checking the property.

"Ma'am, sir, we're really sorry to disturb you, but could you please step inside with us? It's much safer." They always obliged. "My partner and I," Adam continued inside, gas mask still on, "are here for your safety. Please, take a seat." Their nervous faces nodded in unison and they sat on a long white leather couch underlit by soft blue bulbs. The living room was large, with a Positronics Plasma Replicator in the corner and a Daedalus Molecular Printer on the kitchen counter. The Plasma Replicator allowed the user to physically interact with digital environments by rendering holograms over matching molds of interactive, instantly generated nano-plasma. The couple had even bought the Fair Work Version, as evidenced by the small three leaf symbol on the bottom, meaning all materials and labor were ethically sourced. Adam wondered what games they had before continuing. "My partner's currently performing a basic safety check of your property—for free—and she'll be finished in just a minute, so please don't be alarmed." The couple shared a glance. Despite Adam's professionalism, the house registered their anxiety and dimmed the lights to a soft gray-blue and began playing a digital mashup of nature sounds and Vivaldi's Four Seasons.

Kaley walked around and shut windows, turned off the domestic climate controllers, and had to tamper with a digital control panel a bit to kill the air filtration system, but soon she stopped all air flow in and out of the house. She took the tank from her shoulders, set it on the floor around the corner from the couple and quietly opened the nozzle.

"As you can tell, just by looking out the window of your *lovely* home, the world isn't quite as, as safe as it used to be." They both smiled weakly at the compliment and nodded. "And I can tell that, by your *excellent* taste in home furnishings," another smile and nod, "that you're two *very* discerning individuals." The man's shoulders straightened and his wife patted his thigh twice. "So, I assume, you're most likely interested in maintaining this excellent lifestyle." The couple nodded, the woman's head dropping ever so slightly more than her husband's. "Are you aware then," Adam continued, unshouldering his tank and putting his bag on the floor. He left his mask on.

Kaley sat on the couple's bed and made a fist in front of her left eye then extended all fingers, activating her Positronic Media Lens. She used an index finger to flip through news stories of extravagant suicides from Vegas to Vancouver and the ongoing food shortages that gripped the East Coast.

"Of the Wealth Retention Act?" The wife's head cocked in interest and her husband blinked, slowly, shaking his head. They both nudged forward. "Well," Adam said, sitting on a chair that matched the couch. "To avoid seizure of assets, all residential couples between the ages of 25 and 45 must have a child. At least by the time the average age of the couple reaches 28."

"I've heard about this," the wife said, turning to her husband who put his arm around her. "Kareem was saying we can get fined 5% of the total value of all our assets per quarter, unless we prove conception." She turned and pointed at Adam. "You must be from one of those—"

"What if, what if we can't like, get pregnant?" The husband cut her off as Adam nodded.

"Then you'll both see a treatment specialist, appointed by the State." Adam answered. He always marvelled at how well the State handled cases like those.

The couple launched into conversation, saying things Adam had heard too many times to care. He looked around their home, admiring everything the young couple had amassed or inherited. The business partners sat patiently while the romantic couple went back and forth for about ten minutes. Soon they were slurring words and their heads were dropping between syllables.

"Furthermore," Adam sighed as he spoke, interjecting and crossing his legs. "Due to the recent, uh, you know, conflagrations that've been all but uncontrollable,"

"Uh huh," they both muttered, shoulders bent, eyelids drooping, trying to follow what he said.

"The need for fire insurance has grown exponentially," he spoke slowly and even after both of them leaned back and were completely unconscious, kept speaking. "Hence my partner and I offering this free consultation on behalf of go fuck yourself limited, a multinational conglomerate of convoluted subsidiaries and other corporate bullshit that you trust fund cunts know nothing about." He sighed and waited a minute, then stood and slapped their knees. He rubbed their faces then stuck his finger in the husband's nose and wiped the snot on his wife's upper lip.

"Kaley!" She put her phone away and walked in. They moved the furniture to open up more space. The wife they laid on her back, husband on his side, and removed their pants and underwear.

The following twelve hours were a choreographed and most profitable routine. Every thirty minutes each subject was given an injection to stimulate their reproductive systems—she'd start mass producing eggs as the lining of her ovaries was thinned, and his testicles would become engorged with semen. Every forty-five minutes Kaley would lubricate a plastic glove and insert a thumb and start massaging the prostate while a plastic device was secured over the penis.

While she was doing this, Adam set the scene. He took two wine glasses from the cupboard and pressed them to their lips and into their palms. Then he opened two bottles of wine and after taking two big swigs, poured a bit in each glass then swirled it about to coat the insides. He emptied the bottles in the sink, leaving one there and the other on the floor near the two glasses He spread some snacks on the table—smoked salmon leftovers, a can of caviar, a sleeve of organic gluten free multi-grain crackers which he tossed on a small plate with slices of cured ham and a slab of gouda cheese. After deciding it looked real enough, he took a glass from the sink, filled it, and drank the entire thing in long, full gulps. He walked into the living room to see Kaley thumbing the stranger's asshole with detached but professional vigor.

"Having fun?" he asked, fishing crumbs from his teeth. She smirked and gave him the finger with her free hand.

"I still can't believe we discontinued those APMs. Made my life so much easier."

"The automatic massagers? They caused fucking cancer!"

Kaley held her free hand out, palm up and waved it about, as if gesturing to the whole world. "Like it fucking *matters?*"

"You have no business sense." Adam shook his head and walked over to prod the wife's distended belly with a finger before injecting her again. He looked over at the Plasma Replicator and smiled. After opening the nozzle and checking the gauge on his tank, he stepped onto the platform and started flipping through the holographic menu that popped up.

"You poured out *all* the wine?" Kaley asked, walking back from the kitchen, rubbing sanitizer into her hands. Adam didn't respond. He was in a boxing match with the Pope Urballn Stephen VI, who was a Hungarian doctor and ex-drug dealer, throwing jabs that landed with meaty slaps. Adam danced backwards, saw the Papal Tiara he'd knocked off a minute ago on the mat of the ring and kicked it. The Pope flew at him in a rage.

"Well," he dodged twice, threw a hook, missed. "You gotta fly, remember?" The round ended and his visor was fogged. "Safety first." Kaley sighed and sat on the couch, opening her Lens again, waiting for the husband's refractory period to end. Adam ended the match and found a drones-eye view of a rooftop sauna in Japan, and after switching from plasma to hologram display, scaled the image up and tossed it in front of Kaley.

"Perv," she said while swiping it back. He shrugged and

kept switching angles until he was looking from the eyes of one of the women. He switched the interactive plasma display back on and after an hour, his neck was cramped from looking down and both his wrists were sore. The wife still wasn't ready, so he explored the sea floor instead.

Three hours later he inserted a long ultrasound probe into her vagina. He pressed one of six buttons on the device and a holographic image of her ovaries appeared. After tweaking the image a bit he extended a thin hollow tube into an ovary. Another button began the process of removing the eggs, which were deposited in a small pouch that rested between her thighs. "Red gold," he said, watching it fill up. "Red, fucking, gold." He repeated the process on her other ovary then put the product in a climate controlled pouch in the duffle bag he'd carried in.

The team posed the couple in a sensual arrangement after removing more of their clothes and tossing them about, then put a few snacks around their bodies. Finally, the last stage of the consultation, ensuring these strangers would become customers. "So," Paul said, injecting the husband just below the navel, sterilizing him. "About those burgers."

"Hm," Kaley responded, doing the same to the wife. "Kinda feeling pasta now."

Paul shrugged. "Figure it out on the flight back?" Kaley nodded.

"Gonna go get her warmed up," she said, grabbing her empty tank and putting the needles, gloves and lubricant into her bag.

Paul walked into the kitchen, had another bite of caviar, tossed a red and black business card in a drawer full of miscellaneous junk, then took a folded piece of manila paper from his bag and slid it under a magnet on the side of the refrigerator. The first line read, *If you care about your future, please read the following with great care.*

The night is cold and there is no light

The night is cold and there is no light.
I pedal through my solitude and
over rock-laden grass that
jostles screws loose on my bike.

A helicopter passes overhead and
hovers a hundred yards away.
It amazes me and my drunken unimportance.
In my drunken bravery I pedal

towards the airborne wealth. My path
is blocked by a fence blocking
a river. I stand, rip
my gloves off, and in my drunken

genius, piss on my gloves.
I want to punch myself in the face and
almost do, but instead tighten
the screws on my bike.

I get home and write uneventful poetry,
watch free porn involving
baseball bats, eat my roommate's leftovers.
My nights are cold and there is no light.

Cavalcades of questions. All we had to do was look down

Day Job

I slam the door shut in the dead night and run. Everyone does. I'm the fastest, but the suitcase's dense contents, full of life and opportunity, weigh me down.

The holdup itself was easy—flawless. I ditch my mask on the front porch. The suitcase is under my arm, pressed against my heaving chest. Panic surges through me but the brilliance of shining headlights smothers the cramps and burning legs. I start to sweat.

Five of us sprint down Bradwick St. with long strides that look ridiculous in the shadows of the three street lights. I hear an engine trying to roll over and praise Barry for calling Stephan just as we left the room to give us a head start. I wonder briefly if Barry will get out of there alive and my chest cramps, then the car kicks into life and the loud snap of doors unlocking releases pressure in my heart.

I hop in the passenger seat, the other four pile in back. I slam the suitcase between my feet and Stephan cringes, silently begging me to be careful. I surrender a straight-faced glance and a slight nod, letting Stephan know everything is fine while reminding him that he is still The Driver for this run. The car speeds off and dark seizes my vision as the streetlights fade into the unreasonable night. I exhale slowly and I'm jostled in my seat, the engine coughs and I hope it's going to hold through the concoction of home distilled alcohol and watery diesel.

Three years after Obama's fourth term and his assassination, only the professionals survive. Anyone not affiliated with anyone else, not involved in the food, medicine, gas or sex trade either starves to death, is caught up in the crossfire, or suffers their sickness in the lonely caverns of their home.

The pistols waiting under my arms remind me to be confident and fearless at all times. I'm not a professional, but I act like one.

I look behind me at my four cramped affiliates and see panic in their blotchy faces. Hear fear in their wheezy breathing. They've never done anything like this before, stealing cargo as precious as this, stealing from the Bordwells. They're the only syndicate large enough to levy taxes, enforce their collection with lone wolf third parties and pump out propaganda to compete with the State. I cross my arms and grasp the cold metal on my side, reminding myself why I'm doing this, thinking about how the four in back are getting paid, if it's on them.

Stephan has driven us four or five blocks from the house and I'm still slammed into the back of my seat, oddly disconnected from the feat just accomplished, when engines behind us detonate into life. Packs of lions are starting the hunt. The sound of the engines grows as they gain speed, closing the distance of our head start. The streets are void of any traffic, gutted cars and the Bordwell's leaflets denouncing the State and Project Apeiron are the only residents of the street. I have no idea what kind of cars they're driving, but they are louder and faster than anything I've ever heard and the only thing I can think of is a baby gazelle sprinting in vain from a lioness.

Four pops, the back window starred, screams, two different pitches. Silence from the other two—in shock—engines growling louder. My mind unbuckles along with my seat belt and I dive halfway in the back, pull a screaming and bleeding dirty-blonde girl by the front of her shirt so she is almost doubled up on herself. I feel around her waist, under her arms, and run my palm over her chest and stomach. Her hands are talons that don't help. I find a hole in the small of her back and notice her belly swelling up—she's hemorrhaging.

Blood spills out of her mouth as her wet hands grasp me in her last vibrant thrash of life, acting with a frantic urgency that always makes my throat clench up. More pops, no screams, Stephan pushing the car to its limits. I hear glass breaking and something snap, more pops. The growls are closer still.

I push the girl back into her seat, detach myself mentally from her to try and get a hold of the middle aged Asian man who's been hit in the neck and ear, but she is still set on getting my attention, hoping I can save her. I can't get a grip on the man to her left, he's too far away, and the other two affiliates just sit there with open jaws and clenched hands, eyes wide and struggling to breathe. The girl won't stop. I kick my legs around and connect with the suitcase. *It's there, it's safe.* Reason takes hold and the calmness of action overcomes me as I grasp the cold metal underneath my right arm, pull, and point at the dirty blonde girl. Still frantic. Still the roars.

I pull hard on her shirt and push the barrel under the chin. The writhing body is momentarily still as it's caught in the tension. A muffled *blup* and the back windshield is covered in a splash of a red and pink and white mist as a hole is punched through it and the roaring explodes into the car, waking up the other two who finally close their mouths and realize what is going on. I holster my pistol and glance at the gurgling Asian man, bidding him a silent farewell.

I sit back in my seat and see Stephan talking wildly to himself, the roars drowning out all noise. I turn back around and roll the window down, pull my upper body out, left arm leading with my pistol, and begin pulling the trigger as fast as I can. The kick is tremendous and the wind rips around me, tossing my arm at wild angles.

I pull back in, roll the window up. Stephan still talking to himself. Driver's side mirror gone. Silence in back. *That's why the Bordwells had only fired a handful of rounds: we're driving too fast to make any accurate shots. They're following us. We have to make the drop somewhere, and they know this.*

We still have about a twenty minute drive. Stephan's mouth stops moving, and he looks at me full on, speeding down a dead highway after maneuvering through the eerie streets of Newtown. "We don't have an escort. We gotta lose them on our own." I see the small plastic bulb hooked onto his ear. A Bluetooth. He has been on the phone the entire time.

"Let's uh," I pause, rubbing my face. "Let's take'em through the yards?"

He nods. Stephan is a professional. The other two in back, though still alive, are useless. Dead to me. Stephan knows that this suitcase sitting between my legs is bigger than both of us. Bigger than our paltry payments of sugar or booze, or our allowance of women and drugs, more important than this new dogfight with the Bordwells. We have mouths to feed.

I crack my window to let the wind splash my face. The roar becomes part of the audible scenery, but I never ignore it. Nights with no moon make everything look the same. Even the graffiti is bland and lifeless, the fist with a single raised index finger is everywhere, too large to be ignored, too big to be completely covered. One finger, one solution. It's been the State's symbol for the past three or four years.

Stephan slouches a bit, keeping the car weaving back and forth in irregular patterns. More intermittent pops, aimed only at reminding us to pay attention to the thunder. I'm glad there's silence in the back.

"You holding, by any chance?" I ask.

"Yeah," Stephan answers. "Of course. In the glove compartment."

I reach down and push plastic tabs that border a three digit combination lock.

"It's locked."

Without taking his eyes off the road Stephan reaches down, puts his palm over the lock, rotates the correct numbers in and pops the glove compartment open. Staring back at me is a half-full plastic bottle with a white label and the word 'sambuca' scrawled across it in stenciled font. Stephan got the same paycheck that I did. A whole crate of this and just enough bread and butter to not be distracted by the hunger. I wonder if we got the same share as I twist the cap off and hold the bottle to my lips.

Liquid licorice pours down my throat, the delicious sting melting the thunder from behind. A second gulp and the speeding car isn't slamming me into my seat.

I did what I had to with the dirty-blonde girl. She was headed off anyway, there was nothing I could have done, it's not like there is a hospital for her to be dropped off at. I add her to the uncounted but constantly pondered tally of faces and voices I've kept since I joined the profession. Another sip and her face blurs in my mind as she finishes bleeding in back. I squeeze my knees against the suitcase. *Two lives for a hundred, maybe more, is a victory. I gulp twice. People like me, people who were the working class but are now the fighting class, operate without a conscience while at their job. Thinking about it like that, there isn't much of a difference between then and now, but that seems like the only thing that's stayed the same.*

I take another sip and a wave of speculation jars my mind, rushing up through my reality of the men with guns who are chasing me, trained to retrieve what is theirs and give me the same treatment as those still and silent behind me. I think about how we won't be able to use this car again and almost vomit. The bout of nausea surges through my stomach and my mouth begins to water, I wish in vain to exist only as a body, a machine of moving flesh and bone and nerve with no possession of morals or regret. I screw the cap back on and Stephan removes the bottle from my hands and slides it into a small compartment on his door after taking a lengthy swig. He never takes his eyes off the road. The uncertainty of night embraces me as I yearn for the past like a man dying of thirst.

This is my life. This is our life. We created this. The days of office jobs—complaining about benefits, health care, why the New Guy got the corner office instead of you—that is extinct. Never to return. The satisfaction of trivial things shriveled and ashen like the trees and the flowers. The ogre of my Rationality is in a boxing match with Hope. Hope, barely able to keep its arms up. Rationality, sneering, dancing around with clever eyes.

People should not be dying for this suitcase. I grip my face with both palms as I realize and understand the sacrifice I made. *I pulled that trigger.* I took the life of one in hope that the lives of many would be saved. *Was this instinct? Was this necessary? How many more?*

Another tsunami of nausea obliterates my inner debate and I hold the sambuca back with immense effort, faking a cough. Stephan looks at me, realizes nothing has come up, and looks back at the road.

Sitting in this car with the barrel of my gun still warm is not the time to doubt what I'd done. Like Burc said: predators don't live in the past. *We're still moving, I'm still breathing, I don't have time for it. This is business. Dirty-Blonde is another martyr for the (necessary? arbitrary? perceived?) Greater Good.*

The sambuca speaking for me, I take a breath, and without looking at Stephan ask him "Why do we—?"

Four pops, my mirror shatters, a tire hit.

Stephan, both hands on the wheel, maintains general control. He glances at the rear view mirror then back at the road, eyes squinting, trying to make out something in the distant night. He turns onto an exit labeled E/I 395. We'll be able to ditch the car soon.

"Hey!" I shout into the back.

One responds with a mumble, an odd whimper, another with a higher pitched voice manages to respond with "Yeah?"

"Do you have any weight on you?" A professional question.

One doesn't respond, the other takes a breath and quickly responds, "Yeah."

"Okay, good."

"There's a lot of blood back here." I don't know what to say. Professionals don't care about blood. "A lot."

But I'm also not sitting in the back seat. "Okay, good. That's good." I feel bad, but just don't know what else to say. "Just sit tight bud." Stephan is sweating as he manages to keep the car straight.

A shriek escapes the silent one, a sound of absolute terror and I realize that he's completely normal by the old standards. Not prone to violence, doesn't pick fights, is generally passive or non-aggressive. He is not fit for this life of savagery. He is a bystander, a face in a crowd. He is now scarred.

"Are we hitting the dr-drop soon?" Asks the one who remembers how to speak. I can hear in his voice the distraction caused by the affiliates.

"Yeah." I want to tell him how long, to get ready, that he'll be out of the car and the blood and away from the gore soon. I'm slumped down in my seat and reloading my pistol. "We're close." There is some shuffling and I hear a pistol being handled. I hear more movement, a few clicks as a safety is adjusted, readjusted, and a bullet loaded into a chamber.

I hear the Backseat Gunslinger say something but can't hear it. I roll the window down and let four lead stars escape my clenched fist, aimed at nothing. The rushing wind is soothing and the ringing in my ears reminds me what it's like to be alive, to sense and feel, to live outside my mind and in my body.

A quick series of right turns and a looping left let me know we are almost there. The car's vibrating and the back left tire is almost gone.

"Are you buckled?" I ask.

"No," he clears his throat.

"Good. Are the other three impairing your movement much? You'll need some space coming up."

A respite, two muffled pops, a cold answer. "No."

I squeeze the handle, check how many bullets are left in the clip—twelve—and ready another one.

Why the fuck did he do that? The silent one might have gotten in the way, but—wait, no, you were the one who spoke as if he was already dead. You made the same decision as the Backseat Gunslinger, he just acted on it. He would have gotten in the way, just like Dirty Blonde, if I let her live. The whimperer wasn't even able to speak, him acting or fighting to save his own life, let alone contribute, simply wasn't in the picture. The Backseat Gunslinger did the right thing.

I don't want it to be, but it's endearing.

I turn and empty the clip blindly, reload, pick up the suitcase and hug it tightly.

The powder that is double wrapped in thin plastic and covered in taped newspaper could turn a profit that would shatter my shackles of murder and commitment to a cause I wasn't sure of anymore. I hug tighter, think of where the powder is actually going, take a deep breath and know this is what has to be done.

Stephan swerves through the narrow streets, his white knuckles on the wheel telling me how he feels.

"As soon as you feel the car starting to brake, *hold on*, and just be ready to ditch. Follow me when we're out," I tell the Backseat Gunslinger as I pull a vest from beneath my seat. Without orders I hold the steering wheel as Stephan grabs his own vest and begins to pull it over his head. The steering wheel rocks back and forth and is slick with sweat.

"So—so no vest for me? What's the deal? Why—"

"You won't need one," I try to assure him, but I don't care if he is scared or not. The answer suffices.

"Get ready." Stephan says.

The street is arching in a slow right turn, and as our car reaches the apex of the curve, Stephan whips the wheel to the right and slams the emergency brake and we're skidding, our car almost perpendicular to the Bordwells. We slide down to the floor. Three pops, another blown tire, a starred windshield and two wet thumps. I hear the backseat gunslinger retch as more blood and passenger make their way onto him. I open the door but hold it closed as Stephan punches the accelerator in reverse, and as we turn completely around, facing the Bordwells, Stephan throws the high beams on while backing into a long driveway bordered with short but steep grass hills.

We don't even come to a stop and I'm out. I see Stephan reach out of his window and toss a canister toward the pops and roars, smoke billowing out. We're silhouetted by the high beams. I run. I don't know if the Backseat Gunslinger is following or not until we pass through six or seven backyards and I hear him panting.

I keep sprinting and we are almost at the drop. Two blocks away and the pops are coming in short bursts. Some people are coming out of their houses, their wheezing matching ours, thinking the smoke is a fire, adding to the confusion, but most are of the more intelligent kind, staying in their houses and pretending like nothing is happening. The pops don't stop. I know Stephan is fine.

About six blocks away from the driveway, I slow to a walk in front of a red set of doors that lead into a basement. There are three separate chains, three separate, massive locks keeping everything unwanted out. I pick up one lock and remove it and the chain it's keeping company. I can feel the awkward surprise of the Backseat Gunslinger as he realizes the lock is a fake. I can feel it multiply as I take off the second fake lock.

The basement is the first stage of our processing system, a network of underground production and distribution. I slide the key into the final, actual lock, thinking about how I would describe what we did to the Backseat Gunslinger, ready to incorporate him into our organization as a reward for this run, and how this basement was only a small but vital part of an entire orchestra of—

A pop, fire, burning raging spreading fire, anger, falling, a flood of worry dampening but not dousing the fire.

"Gimme the case." The gun is shaking in his hand, and he doesn't realize he can just take the suitcase resting under my arm. Most of my left kneecap is gone, shot out from behind, shot out by this Backseat Gunslinger. "You guys are fuckin' nuts for pulling this shit on the Bordwells," he shakes his head and his face is cut with a nervous smile. The barrel of his gun is trembling. "Gimme the case."

I try to respond but I'm trapped in my mind, drowning in a billion thoughts, driven by adrenaline, fear for my life, concern for the powder, shame for failing to make the drop, shame for letting this amateur get the better of me, shame for letting this Backseat Gunslinger bring down so much that had been created in this world so far gone.

"You don't even—"

"*Gimme the fuckin' case!*" He stands three feet away, still not realizing he can step forward and take it. "Look, I don't even know why you guys would steal some shit like that. Fuckin' idiots. Like you'd be able to sell all of it anyway?"

Now it makes sense to me. Understanding rushes through me like a winter sunrise.

"You're an idiot. You don't know what—"

"Hey, *hey*, fuck you buddy. *Fuck you.* Who's the one who's shot, huh? Who's the one bleeding, who's the newest member of the c-cripple club, huh? That's right." He starts pacing a bit, gun still shaky. He is instantly drunk on power and out of his mind. There must have been a lot of blood in the backseat. There are smears of gore and flesh on his chest and arms, most of the blood on his face must have melted off from him sweating. "You," he taunts, taking a half step forward and steadying his grip. "Gimme the fucking coke, moron."

I give him a blank stare and forgive him for being so stupid, for being naïve and greedy, for doing this. Burc also said you don't punish ignorance, you cure it. I accept the pain but not the implications of it. I wait for him to pull the trigger like he did in the car. I wish he would finish the job and let me die.

The Backseat Gunslinger, finally fed up, snarls and takes a step forward. He grabs the case. I feel empty and numb with it not in my arms. "Four seven zero one zero eight."

"What?" He is fumbling with the case. "What did—say it again."

"Four seven zero one zero eight." I hear him repeat the numbers slowly to himself as he adjusts the combination lock, kneeling on the ground. I thank Barry again, our inside man, for supplying not only the combination, but the inside lane on the Bordwells.

The Backseat Gunslinger snaps the case open and begins pawing at the double wrapped powder. He's an amateur.

I can kill him right here, the weight of my guns unfelt, a part of my body. It's not my place to punish him. I want him to suffer through this, I want him to cure himself.

I hear ripping sounds as he gets past the first layer of paper. Silence as he peels away the plastic. He dabs his pinky on his tongue and brings it to the powder, then back to his tongue. Confusion, anger, rising anger, exploding anger, simple rage.

"Flour!? Fucking flour!? Are you fucking—"

Pop. The Backseat Gunslinger's face disappears in a fine pink mist. I only think about how the one opened package is now tainted and unusable.

Stephan steps forward and I can see despair creep into his face when he sees me.

"He only opened one package, the rest is still good. I'm fine, just my leg."

Stephan puts the story together himself as he takes the opened package of flour and spreads it over the dead body. It looks like a trillion stars amidst the green and brown grime that used to be grass. He closes the case and jumbles the combination. He rubs his chest, then places the suitcase in my hand and squeezes my fingers around the handle. there is no need to tell me to hold on and there are no inquiries into what happened.

There will be time later. Stephan is a professional.

"Mixing will take a little longer," I croak as he finishes opening the lock and helps me get to my feet.

"Yeah, that's fine. They'll still need bread in the morning."

Our Endowment of Thumbs

We are all masons.
Architects,
brazen bricklayers.

What miracles we construct and obscure.
What do we build for ourselves?

A cistern.
At once our paradise
and our coffin.

The Fishing Boat

It bobs in the small waves
that eat away the shore
to build it elsewhere.
No mast, no oars, no captain.
Just a sway to match the tides
that will someday cease.

The paint is cracked and water
makes its way through once sealed wood
which once was home and sanctuary.

The tides push and pull. Anchored,
the boat respects but doesn't follow them.
For now. The boat remains, and floats.
The rope is strong, but invaded by rot
that is hungry and unstoppable. The rope too
will someday cease.

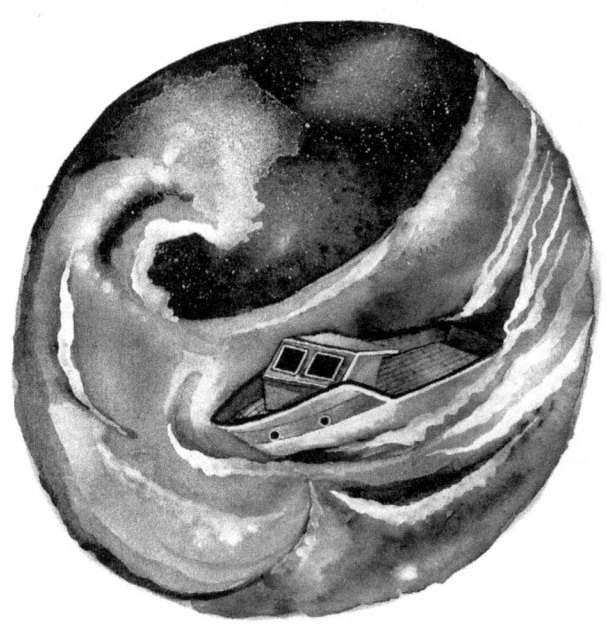

Her Hands Were of Flint and Tinder

And there the island stands
In defiance of the salt god
who is peppered with our unending and unwanted gifts.
Volcanic rock with a scalp soft for roots
that birth homes for many and fuel for few.

The shore is rocky and the distance great,
but the prize of fruit and fuel may match the journey.
A woman with wild tales and rambling hair wades in.
She knows there are sharks, an undertow, and jellyfish.
She smiles and dives over a cresting wave.

The salt god responds and the waves flex
but the woman knows to kick, stroke, breathe.
The ocean is vast and tireless.
She fights slow and smart
and will not stop

for the shore is aflame
and the island her only salvation.

after a certain age
the shadows that hide our future

The Nest
lose their adventerous appeal

Sarah Timmins passed the final minutes of math class by shading the bulbous nose of the Frosty Frigate, a spacecraft she imagined speeding along the rings of her notebook. It held 8 passengers, three of which were crew, and was headed to the Alpha Giga Epsilon system, planet EG71—codenamed Gaia—on a routine resupply and transport mission. The crew was double checking cargo to ensure it was secured and the environmental systems were sound. Three scientists and two engineers were recording final messages before they began their eleven month trip in stasis. The captain was about to address the ship when Dr. Dona called attention to the class. Sarah's pencil skipped a beat and punctured the perforated line of her notebook. Hull breach. Pressuring dropping. Oxygen loss. Seal compartment seven.

Dr. Dona lumbered in front of the class from behind the forest of her desk, a brown lamp shedding unnecessary light on hills of papers that made them look aged in the sunlit room. Spectacles hung from a thin silver chain and rested on her blouse, setting sunlight to dance upon the faces of her students. Two canyons of wrinkles fell down from the sides of her nose, each sprouting tiny rivulets of age, contouring her face as rivers sluice through rock over centuries. Her cheekbones were high, much to the dismay of her skin, and even her earlobes seemed to stretch downward.

Under needless fluorescent lights she spoke for the eternity of three minutes about the weekend's homework, the necessity of responsibility, various dangers the future held for those who couldn't finish a geometry worksheet, how they would be in college and beyond soon enough. She paced to the left and right, her lumbering gait practiced and method-ical, as were her measured words, and when the bell rang in the middle of a sentence she shrugged and returned to her hovel. Sarah caught a glimpse of Dr. Dona's calves as she shot her legs out and sat heavily in her black and gray chair. Her skin was pale and ghoulish, reminding Sarah of boiled chicken, and lacing every inch of the massive trunks were fireworks and cobwebs of red and blue veins, some bulging, some recessed, all carrying the ancient sap that kept the Dr. Dona Math Machine functioning.

The class shuffled papers together, slapped their books shut and abandoned their chairs as they sprinted forward, out of their orderly rows and into freedom. Sarah peeked at her legs over the top of her desk and kicked them out, looking past the white fringes of her cut offs that ended just above her knee. Instead of the fireworks and cobwebs of a body rushing toward the soil, she saw the clear skies of youth in her legs.

With nothing packed, Sarah looked up to the mostly empty classroom, the children sprinting toward the infinite opportunities of Friday afternoon. She slammed her textbook shut and tossed it in her bag, slid her pencil into the binding of her notebook and bid farewell to the passengers of the Frosty Frigate. Three steps from the door and Dr. Dona in-formed her that in her youthful haste, her pencil had tumbled to the floor, like a Frosty passenger sucked into the void. Her voice was tired and old and reminded Sarah of the time Dad pulled a dead tree stump from the backyard to clear room for the shed, and the long wet ripping sound the roots made.

"It's okay, you know." Dr. Dona continued as she turned in her chair. The lamp spilled light over her shoulder and ob-scured part of her face. Sarah stopped in the doorway and cocked her head, pulling on the straps of her backpack.

"What is?"

"Your daydreaming, your doodling." Sarah remembered how strong the roots were and how high they stretched into the sky when Dad finally tore it from its home. She imag-ined the longest root tipping into space and crashing into the Frosty Frigate. Catastrophic failure. Confirm deaths and initiate analysis. "Only because of your scores, though." Dr. Dona peered over her glasses. The lamp made her skin look jaundiced. She held a purple marker and someone's assignment like they were a part of her, a branch and a leaf. Her tilted head pushed her chins down and out and Sarah thought of the deep-sea fish she learned about in science earlier in the week: bloated, pink, terrifying, floating at the bottom of the ocean and sucking in anything edible. Dr. Dona turned left and right in her chair just as the fish would in the tiny currents of the pitch black depths.

"Thanks," the child said, smiling politely and taking a half step out the door.

Dr. Dona leaned back, light framing her head, making all but her mouth invisible. "You have a bright future ahead of you," she began, putting the marker and paper down to fold her hands. Sarah swallowed and shifted her weight from left foot to right and back. It had taken Dad half a day to finish. "In a lot of ways, too." Dr. Dona stretched a limb out to adjust a small black pigeon statue on her desk, pointing its head toward Sarah.

"What do you mean?" Sarah nibbled her lower lip and Dr. Dona swung her trunks under her desk then removed her simple shoes to rest her feet on the floor. She stared out the window and looked at the oak trees as they leaned back and forth then side to side in the wind. She rubbed her hands together and squinted her eyes as if trying to discern some magical truth from their movement.

"I've been doing this for a long time," she leaned back and held both palms out and opened her arms as if gesturing to the whole world. "And after a while, you begin to learn certain things, see things in people they may not see themselves." Dr. Dona turned and looked at Sarah but her face was still obscured, and now her hair looked like a million snakes as she slumped down in her forest colored chair. "You, you're a very smart young woman, and the world needs women like you." She cleared her throat and Sarah thought of the slow thump the tree made when it was finally defeated. "You have great things ahead of you, but you need to understand they won't be handed to you. Especially with how you'll look."

The child licked her lips and nodded, eyes darting away.

"Do you understand what I'm saying?"

"Of course, Doctor. It really means a lot. I'll be sure to finish *all* my homework—" The words tumbled out of her but were cut short by a lumbering wave of a hand that came to rest on a stack of blue, red and yellow folders.

"I know you will," Dr. Dona picked up her marker and turned back to her desk, the lamp obscuring her silhouetted profile. "Enjoy your weekend."

"I will. B-bye Dr. Dona." Sarah said as her teacher shuffled from side to side, getting comfortable and putting her shoes back on.

Dr. Dona looked up from her desk and again the only thing Sarah could see was her mouth. "Okey doke. See you on Monday." A smile opened across Dr. Dona's face and the limestone bricks of her teeth made Sarah laugh uncomfortably and spill more non-committal thanks from her mouth before escaping the quicksand pit of the after school talk. She walked fast down the empty hallway, pulling out her hairband to retie her ponytail in a tight bun, but she couldn't get all her hair in her haste, so a few errant strands spilled in front of her eyes. The lockers blurred into a gray mass as she ran, light that spilled from classrooms punctuated the hallway, her footsteps echoed long and loud through the empty school.

To exit Vernon Hill elementary school's front doors, you have to pass through a foyer with a set of small marble stairs. On either side of this room two old murals greeted you or wished you farewell. Sarah always took her time going through so she could stare at the massive paintings, to wonder who painted them, how long it took, what they were wearing when they made them, what snacks they were munching on between strokes. One was of a family, a stout mother in a pale blue bonnet and matching dress who knelt in the back of a wooden carriage with a child on her hip. She pointed forward but looked at her three other children who were sitting across from her. Sarah wondered what they looked like, if they liked sports or makeup, or both. Or if they had sports or makeup at all. All of them were clad in blue coats with colonial-era white lapels and three point hats. Their father, grim faced, was dressed the same with a musket in his lap and leather straps wrapped around his wrists that he gripped with great intensity. But the details of the family weren't what struck Sarah this time. She stared instead at the horses the man held the reins to.

Three massive noble beasts humbled by their harnesses, bound forever to do the bidding of their owners. Their white manes burst like trails of flame from their bronze backs, the detail of the muscles incredible, their power conveyed perfectly. They would haul and carry and work until their joints failed them, upon which they'd be gifted with a musket ball to the skull for their unerring dedication. Sarah stared into their shining black eyes, one foot hanging in the air above the next stair, one hand on the railing. She'd seen animals show emotion before, her uncle Ronnie had a labrador that would go ballistic if the words "peanut butter" or "outside" were heard, but these animals, despite the obvious skill of the painter, seemed to have none. Nothing to make them happy, set them on edge or relieve them. A trio that existed merely for their labor, to trudge through the necessary toil they were born into. Their lifeless eyes and battering hooves stayed with Sarah as she hooked her thumbs under the straps of her backpack and cantered down the stairs two at a time. The tall, red and gray doors slammed shut behind her. She couldn't stop thinking about the reins that strapped the horses to the wagon.

Sarah lived an eight minute walk away, but Carpet Mice, her favorite cartoon, didn't start until five o'clock, so she had two and a half hours to get her revenge on Ricky Baron. Last week was the first time they let her play quarterback, and she'd thrown an interception to Ricky who returned it for a touchdown, juking her to the ground in the process. The grass stains took two days to come off her wrist and knees.

She turned left and walked toward the field when she saw Kelly, Jess and Madison sitting on the edge of the garden in front of the school. Kelly, blonde hair in perfect pigtails with a blue and yellow polka-dotted dress, was talking and gesturing with something small and black in her hand. Jess listened intently as the wind kicked up her straight black hair. Madison was tapping away on her pink phone when Kelly twisted the plastic and unscrewed it from itself, revealing a pink tip. Kelly dabbed it on her lips three times then rubbed them together, demonstrating what her fifteen year old sister had taught her.

The small black stick was passed around and the process repeated, each of them admiring each other's work. As she walked by, Sarah wrinkled her brow in curiosity, and in that moment Kelly glanced up. The look was matched by a curled lip and rolling eyes, then a lean and whisper that made the trio look and laugh at the same time. The interception evaporated and Sarah walked quicker, pressing her lips into a small straight line.

The field was cut right out of a small forest that surrounded the school. The swath of flat, bright green was jarring but welcome, a casual invitation amidst the limbs of oak and birch. The trees were alive in the wind, swaying with slow breathing and a song only they could sing, a song of layered shadows and beckoning old age. Sarah passed through the chain-link gate immune to the ancient melody, hearing instead cries for the ball, taunting and energetic yelling, the growing calls to organize teams. She dropped her bag and joined the group, waiting for the ball to soar her way. A few kids were racing up and down the fields with thin, darting legs.

Davide Greene eventually shouted her name and launched the ball in a high arc that sent Sarah sprinting underneath it. Her calculation was perfect but her footing wasn't. The football fell into her cupped arms as she tumbled over herself in a mess of limbs and grass, the ball crushing her solar plexus and exhausting every bit of air from her lungs. Everyone saw it as a great catch instead of a fall, but their cheers didn't return anything to her lungs so she took her time getting to her feet. Her temples throbbed. Her face burned red. Her chest was a knot that refused to loosen. She only lasted a few steps before holding up a finger and taking a knee. The first breath brought the voices of the trees and boys back, whispers from the ancient and shouts from the young, the second and third breaths brought the life back in her step, and after the sixth she launched the ball to Bradley, who scrambled to get under it, only to drop it. Sarah didn't care about the bad throw. That catch was *amazing*.

Jason, the fastest, and Chris, the tallest, refused to be on the same team. Each wanted bragging rights over the other. They were captains and everyone fell in line before them, waiting to be judged and picked. The first three picks by each captain were rapid with no pause between the name calling. The latter half took more deliberation. Sarah was picked tenth out of sixteen, better than the dead last of last week. Endzones were set and the teams walked off in separate directions, quietly discussing plays and coverages amidst non-stop trash talk. Friendships suspended themselves and the cohesion of a team set in place, a unity that nurtured the unabashed competition and glory of playground sports.

The score was rabid and discipline elusive, rules negotiated and renegotiated, amazing displays of dexterity were followed by gangly elbow flopping and knee tangling. Sarah caught six or seven passes and two touchdowns, one was in traffic where she put some moves on Bradley and the other a picturesque comet that floated into her hands as she exacted her revenge and torched Ricky, beating him into the endzone by a full three strides. Her team had a substantial lead, but there is no quit in sixth grade sports. On a failed reverse, Sarah was trying to block and create a lane for Jason but instead caught a shoulder to the jaw from Sean, opening up the inside of her cheek. She hawked blood and spit it out. The glob of silent pride landed on the white out of bounds line. His immediate concern and her shaking her head with palms up was their only discussion, an instant reconciliation.

The game ended and those with the late afternoon curfew began their sprint home, the shadows of the trees singing after them but growing tired with the failing light. Sarah tongued the cut in her cheek and walked to her bag, staring into the trees. An urge to trudge through the pathless unknown rushed through her and she almost rode the current into whatever may have come when the football thudded some feet to her right. She punted it back, the *whump* of her kick loud and solid. She shouted her goodbyes and headed off the field, shouldering her bag and relishing her fatigue as her adrenaline faded and hunger soared.

The entrance to the field led to a long driveway which fed into a parking lot behind the school. Sarah looked right and thought about taking the scenic route, one that looped behind the school, acorns and leaves scattered about, the stout brick school to her left and the gesticulating trees to her right. Hunger decided for her and she turned left towards the street lined with pale blue, beige and yellow houses. She walked in the gutter, kicking rocks with long strides and leaping over sewer grates, each stone a game winning goal and each jump a spectacular avoided tackle, another highlight to pile on the already massive collection. After launching a fat acorn high and far enough to make her gasp—cars lined either side of the street—she let her breath go in a single gust as a lucky breeze pushed it to the right to land in front of a driveway where it settled next to a dead bird. The bird was mangled and had died in a bizarre position so Sarah couldn't tell what kind it was, but the aftermath of its death made its life seem violent and short. Her phone vibrated in her bag and she slumped one strap off, unzipped and dug her arm in. It was Dad.

"Hey!" She said with a high skip and a smile that was too big for her face.

"Captain Timmins!" She could hear the smile on his face, too. They both had the same slightly too large front teeth. "Are you home yet?"

"Nope, I'm on my—"

"Good, look kiddo—"

"Guess how many touchdowns I caught today!"

He said something she couldn't make out. "Oh, how many strikeouts this time?" he asked. She laughed, wrinkled her brow and smiled at his stupid joke.

"No, *touchdowns*. No one's even thinking about baseball, it's out of season. Guess how..." She could tell someone else was there, someone who had his full attention, someone who was laughing but trying not to.

"Look, stop, gimme a minute. A *minute*, okay?" A whispered order that wasn't directed at her and she knew what was coming next. Her skip died to a slow walk and she glanced at the snapped bird as a few feathers moved in the wind. "Hey, Captain," a door opened and closed. He sighed. "Sarah, look. Hey, are you still there?" She gave him silence because it was the only thing she could. "Sarah?"

"I'm here," she surrendered and let him speak. Words, angry or pleading, never worked here. Neither did tears.

"I won't be able to make it to the lake with you tomorrow." There it was. "Between traffic, Bill getting sick, Nicole forgetting the presentation, the flight being delayed—it all, we all just ran way off schedule and everything turned into a giant mess. Worst business trip ever." Sarah sat on the curb and stared between two houses into the shadows of a patch of trees that moved with the waving bird. She wanted to dive in and disappear. "The boat'll still be there next week." He paused and she could see him, rubbing his temples and trying to think of what to say. "No one's gonna come and snatch up all our fish. The spot for our hammocks isn't going anywhere." He spoke with a steel that reminded Sarah the oars were too big for her. The fish were too strong for her. The hammocks too tall for her to tie. He paused and she wanted to drown in the silence, to be swallowed up by the blackness in the trees, to be cocooned by its shadows and emerge free on the other side of the forest. "I know how ya feel champ. I wanna—"

"*No* you *don't.* You *say* that you do but you *don't.*" Sarah surprised herself with words she would never say to his face. She inhaled to continue but was cut off.

"I'm mad just like you are. I don't want to be here!" He stopped and Sarah could see him running his hand through his hair, ruffling it up in thought and frustration so it stuck out in all directions. After a minute Dad spoke again, his voice was low and sounded like a car driving down a dirt road. "Remember the one with the two top fins? The green stripes? Do you think I'd forget about that fight so easily?" She saw Dad rubbing the scar that was still pink and ran along the soft side of his hand, ending at the base of his little finger. She had hooked the fish, but it was a fight to reel in, even for Dad. They had it out of the water and Sarah was holding the net while Dad danced around the somehow unbroken pole trying to find a good angle to grab it. The fish went wild as soon as Dad's hand got near, cutting the line and his hand with, they thought, it's oddly ridged double fin along its back.

Sarah sighed. It was difficult for her to stay angry, especially at him. She gave him more silence and blinked again and again as the wind let the bird's wing fall. "We gotta get'em," she smiled small and slow, head perched between her knees, staring at dead leaves in the gutter. He laughed and agreed as a door opened and some soft voice said things Sarah couldn't quite make out, things she hated and wanted to burn.

"We still have to finish that game of Risk, too."

"Oh that's right!" This morning she'd accidently bumped into the board, shifting a few of the pieces around. She thought she got them all back where they belonged.

"But listen, you know you're the captain, but let's wait to take out the boat together, okay? Old Twofin doesn't stand a chance against us."

"You know it."

"I'll see you tomorrow night," this was his getting ready to hang up routine.

"Okey doke."

"Don't forget to help Mom with the dishes and clean up after yourself."

"I won't."

"Oh—almost forgot, what are the Vikings up to?"

"Yeah! Actually," she sat up straight and kicked her legs out, thinking. "Lief was born and now he's all grown up. I'm pretty sure he's going to head out to Greenland soon."

"You're coming up on some good stuff pretty soon. Keep me up to date, okay?"

"Yeah, I will. See ya soon."

"I love you, champ."

"Love you too Dad." The phone was heavy in her hand, the screen moist from her face. The victory minutes ago seemed buried in time, blurred and discolored. She started walking. Nothing was added to the lifetime highlight reel. Tired and hungry, Sarah wanted to kick her shoes off and collapse on the couch, to dive into a sea of pillows and thick, old blankets ten times too big for her, to fall asleep watching a movie she'd seen a hundred times so should could wake up and not be lost.

Ankles sore, eyelids heavy, stomach empty, Sarah walked with deliberate slowness, as the oars of a massive Viking ship struck deep into the water and pushed slowly along the sea, so too did her feet drag. Sarah turned right up Fifth Ave and couldn't wait for the comforting drone of Mom's voice, listing the sales she'd made, how cousins and uncles in New York and Nova Scotia were doing, how such and such food was being disagreeable for making it difficult for her to do such and such thing to it.

At the end of Fifth Avenue was a single family house with old white paint, nonfunctional black matte shutters and a gray shingle roof. The two houses on either side were similar, nondescript homes. Behind them was a forest, the same one that used to stretch through the town and be one with the trees by the school, but was torn down in the name of suburbia. The tops of these trees reached above the roof, giving the house a thorny crown, but because the house sat on a small hill, the closer Sarah walked the smaller the thorns became. The small front yard was well kept, the grass well-cared for, a small white gazebo surrounded by bushes and covered with vines on the right, a sycamore sapling not fifteen years old claiming its own space on the left. Hibiscus and red lantanas framed the border of the yard, planted in fresh brown-red mulch. Sarah loved when Mom planted candy cane striped Dahlias or carnations along this border because they always looked so beautiful together, especially since Mom kept a meter of cottongrass just behind them. The earthy smell was the first sign of home, the first wave of an aura that made her breathe deep and smile. She waded through the front door and was about to yell hello when she heard Philip Glass playing from speakers in the kitchen and Mom talking something business to someone on the phone. Sarah could tell by the ice in her voice.

She let her shoulders droop and her backpack slid off as she walked to the end of the couch. When her thighs hit the armrest she fell forward, tipping over and landing in absolute comfort. She grabbed her hair band and pulled, freeing her dark brown hair. Slowly, with great fatigue and pleasure, she scratched her scalp with grimy fingernails. Her teeth felt rusty with the day and remains of the game clung to her skin. She loved the feeling of being tired and dirty when she got home, it made her feel like she'd accomplished something, like she had grabbed the world and had a good tussle with it. She groaned and every want reverberated with that sound. Just as she rallied enough to push herself off the couch, the weight of tomorrow's fishing trip pushed her back down. She sighed and closed her eyes, falling into her sadness and letting it wash over her like muddy water.

They'd talked about that trip for weeks. She pushed her face into the cushion, wanted to scream and almost did. She sighed instead.

Music from the kitchen, the patter of Mom's feet, her shuffling papers and spirited voice, all mingled to make Sarah embrace the calmness of home. Plays from the game ran through her mind and she smiled.

She clenched her jaw then leaned on her elbows. "No," she said to herself, pushing herself to her knees and letting the murky water fall from her skin. "I'm going." She looked around at the room and hummed along to the Violin Concerto and thought how impossible it would be for Mom to say no after a pre-emptive chores attack. Papers, a glass on the table, her backpack, a blanket at the end of the couch, the shoes by the front door, all lying about. And this was just the living room. She hopped off the couch, everything that had a home she brought there, anything out of place was returned to the way it needed to be, and in a few minutes she was finished. She looked around and thought, *There's always something that needs to be done.* Time to tackle the kitchen and Mom in business mode. Peeking around the corner she saw mom slide onto a stool from the side.

The chairs on either side of the kitchen table were made of the same pale yellow birch as the table itself, which came up to Sarah's chest, the marble counters and black stove the same height. The upper cabinets and certain parts of the fridge still required her humbling stepstool. The speaker was at the far end of the kitchen and she wanted to hop up and change the song to the man who kept screaming about how good he feels, when another idea slowed her feet and brought a cat-like posture to her shoulders.

With long, exaggerated strides Sarah crept into the kitchen, undetected, while Mom grew more agitated with the person she was talking to. Her voice rising then falling, words honed with delicate precision, a surgeon with phrasing and expert dealmaker, it took a mighty wave to rock her boat and knock her off the course she'd taken. Sarah didn't know exactly what she sold, but she did know Mom was really good at it.

Sarah looked at Mom and readied herself for the final approach when the horses from the school mural rose in Sarah's mind like a distant ship returning home, breaking the horizon. The image in her mind looked nothing like what

Sarah saw before her and her feline posture waned as the two incongruous images danced on top of each other. The horses, with senseless intensity in their eyes and froth on their lips, their legs a chaotic mess of movement, Mom with her hair held back in a perfect bun, faint wrinkles around her eyes and falling from the sides of her nose, one hand holding a pen, the other gesticulating in rhythm with her words.

The largest horse looked at Sarah and its face morphed into Grandma's, telling her how she'd grow up to be smarter and prettier than Mom, and she remembered how it was last Thanksgiving when Grandma had said this, and how the compliment was awesome in its potential but impossible in its chances. Sarah shook her head, jostling the images away. She looked at Mom and saw everything she wanted to become, her cheeks taught and mouth firing away, a round nose tipped with pink, long dark eyelashes guarding exuberant eyes, the centerpieces of her animated face. Mom sat at the kitchen table and light poured over her head and shoulders then dripped down her neck and tapered off halfway down her gray tank top. She tilted her head back and closed her eyes, letting the light roll off her cheeks and chin in a baptism of fluorescence.

Sarah dashed forward and clambered to the top of a stool opposite of Mom and stood on it. Her mother's eyes shot wide but her mouth didn't stop as Sarah began her mock ballet, swaying arms and flailing her legs in time with the music. The choreography the primera ballerina showcased was lithe, angelic and punctuated by her signature abstractions. On a single toe she swung her arms wide and high and they grew pale in the light from the ceiling. It was a stunning display of adolescent suppleness that was certain to inspire awe in her maternal impresario.

Instead the stool lurched and her arms thrashed wildly in a failing attempt to fix what was destined to be broken. She was falling and could tell by the angle that it was going to end up a head first affair, a tragically fast terminus for one that showed such promise. She was falling, her eyes closed, waiting for pain and embarrassment and the floor, the end, was rushing up at her when her side was squeezed and she was pulled onto something soft. There was no tumble, only a gasp.

Sarah landed on Mom's stomach and breasts. Mom was on her hip and elbow, holding Sarah and the phone. In breathless pain she managed to wheeze, "One second Paul," before pressing a button and screaming "What are you *doing?* Jesus child, are you out of your mind?" Mom's eyes were a blaze of white and brown. She rocked her hips to move the silent, still child. "Is it a deathwish you have or just no damn—" Sarah's eyes were full and red and she'd retreated as far as she could against the legs of the table, away from her mother's wrath.

"I'm sorry, I'm really sorry, I didn't mean to, I just," Sarah offered but Mom held up her hand and brought her cellphone to her face, shook her head and sighed as she pushed herself to her feet. Mom's face was a full display of anger that left the feline ballet dancer crumpled offstage. After a minute Sarah stood with lowered shoulders.

She wanted to walk into the ocean, to wade out and not stop until she disappeared, swallowed by some eternal current that deposited her in the lightless depths. As she walked out of the kitchen she dragged her fingers across the cabinets, the ones Dad built and took two weeks to install. One of her earliest memories was her parents discussing those blueprints. Mom was holding her just as she finished drawing them and Dad had been so excited to finally see them. The critique and counterpoint was so calm and measured with each syllable so full of love that Sarah felt as if her parents were discussing plans for her future.

The living room was dark and empty, but Sarah still knew what every picture on the wall looked like, knew the contour of every piece of furniture, even where the softest parts of the carpet were, but she didn't want to mingle in a room so full of care and love. She turned left and started the climb to her room. Each stair was a wave bigger than the last and her feet were bricks. Pictures of Grandpa and Grandma lined the wall, the first few captured Grandpa in a world of sepia. Grandpa next to his printing press, another of him standing with his then girlfriend and her first printed book, they both stood tall with smiles that carried happiness through the years. Now the curled lips seeped disappointment, the black eyes that used to fill her with love and ambition now judged her immaturity and thoughtlessness. Sarah rounded the top of the stairs into the hallway decorated with color photographs that brewed a multi-toned disdain that Sarah couldn't comprehend. She leaned her head on her bedroom door and sighed before opening it.

A long mahogany dresser stretched before her, the brass handles Dad put on were still polished, the knick on the edge still bright and obvious. Dirty clothes in a pile in the far left corner next to her window, pale blue curtains doing nothing to stop a flood of red sunlight from spilling all over her floor and bed. A half finished F-16 fighter jet model lay amidst itself just under the window. In the right corner, the board game she now wanted to smash.

She took small steps in and wanted to melt into the forest of thin willow branches and birds that lined the bottom third of her wall, to fall into the cream background and never return. Her eyes moved above the forest and into the deep blue that she had spent weeks decorating, taping pictures and glueing foam models of planets all over the walls and ceiling, trying to recreate the solar system.

She laid face down on her bed and let her head be swallowed by her pillow, and with the brooding patience only a child has, wondered what her punishment would be. Fishing was out of the question. Computer was gone. TV little, if any. She sighed and rolled over, looking out the window and into the blackness of the forest and blood of the sky.

She rolled over again. The immensity of what happened versus what she expected loomed over her like a cresting tsunami so massive it never seemed to move, but she knew it rushed towards her nonetheless. She propped herself up on her elbows and looked at her room, a cluttered city of toys and memories. When Sarah had found out Pluto wasn't a planet anymore, she insisted on taking it from her ceiling. When Dad trotted the ladder out, Sarah was on the second rung before the supports were locked.

Dad stood behind her with arms up, Sarah extended her legs on the top rung, but couldn't reach. She strained and stretched, grunting and wanting so terribly to set the solar system right, but the final three inches would not yield, no matter how hard she tried and how much she wished. Finally instructing her to come down a bit, Dad climbed the ladder and lifted Sarah up into space where she snatched at the once-planet, sneered in effort, finally got an edge of it and began pulling. Sarah never noticed the beads of sweat appearing on Dad's forehead, and since she was shaking with excitement, didn't notice Dad was doing the same with approaching exhaustion.

Pluto eventually came tumbling down, but not without a chunk of the paint. The sticker folded in on itself, disappearing. But the white gash remained, triangular with rounded edges, and Sarah stared at it now, sighing, bringing herself down from the heavens to her forest.

The skylarks, thrushes and robins that were captured in paint along the bottom third of Sarah's wall sang to her. They were beings of freedom trapped. Would they ever be free? Would they grow old and die? A breeze shook the tops of the trees outside Sarah's window while the ones on her wall were still. The interception floated through the mud of her thoughts, but this time it was the pointing and laughing that were dredged up, how her mistake seemed typical and expected. Three girls sneered up from the pits of her mind, but she pushed them back down and tried to swallow the odd fear that rushed up with their red lips. Sarah wondered if a skylark ever wanted to grow up to be a robin, or a robin a thrush. The Viking history book sat closed on her dresser.

Sarah grabbed her blankets and rolled herself over a few times until she faced the edge of the bed. She started a gentle rock, back and forth. Another inch would send her tumbling to the floor, again.

The sun continued to dip. Through her window the child could see all the colors of the world. Orange flames reached up into yellow, blue and purple expanses dotted with the diamonds of Venus and the brightest stars. A wild and unknowable tangle of trees cradled the falling sun, their thin fingers grasping at what was left of the light before succumbing to the darkness. She sighed and swallowed, tasting the infinite solitude of the universe as her cheeks became wet. The two-finned fish swam up through her tears and she decided she would catch it and kill it.

Mom knocked softly three times before opening the door and leaning in. Sarah wanted to be alone but couldn't defy the law. The end of the bed sagged with Mom's weight and her patient silence burned Sarah's shame away.

"I'm sorry I yelled at you like that," Mom said, rubbing her leg. "I really didn't mean to."

"I know. But you were on a work call." Sarah answered after a minute, trying to fill her voice with the cold metal that Dad had.

Mom sighed and squeezed the child's calf. "You scared me! One second I'm talking about delayed shipments and tax refunds and other boring stuff, when the next," she turned and brushed Sarah's hair behind her ear, "there's a jumping, crazy ballerina on top of a kitchen stool!" She ended with a laugh.

"It wasn't *that* crazy," Sarah defended, glancing over with a smirk she failed to hide.

"To you! I mean, it's a good thing I'm taking kickboxing," Mom stood and did twisting knee-jabs and punches, making fake fighting sounds. "Or I never would have been quick enough to save the Captain!"

Sarah leaned up on one elbow, looking at her mother who was kneeling and framed by the window. The setting sun spread a halo around the crown of her head, fading from orange to purple. "The Captain doesn't *need* saving, just so you know."

"Oh-h, that's right! I guess my memory's finally starting to go in my old age. It's a good thing I still have my muscles!" She stood and shadow devoured her face, her arms wrapped around the blanketed child, lifted her with ease and folded her over a shoulder. "She may not need saving now," Mom chanted as she stood, taking extended steps, making Sarah laugh and flop around. "But I'll always be here if she does."

The Mom and the bundle she carried sat at the top of the stairs, both breathing heavy, one from laughter, the other from weight. Sarah's head was pointed down the stairs, laughing, face turning red, trapped in the blanket and held by her feet.

Mom cocked her head. "Hungry?"

Sarah nodded. "For what?"

"Mmm," Mom's eyes rolled all around their sockets. "How about—"

"Pizza!"

"Done! First, do two things for me," Mom asked, the laughter gone from her face. Sarah looked into her eyes, waiting. "One, keep your chin in your chest." Sarah did. "And two, don't tell Dad." Sarah's breath rushed out in a wild scream as Mom slid down the stairs on her butt and back, holding the cocoon of her daughter as they tumbled down in laughter and screams and hitched breathing that ended in a heap of shrieks. After ceremoniously freeing herself from the blankets, Sarah announced: "I wanna call!"

"We need to decide what to order, silly."

"Broccoli! Peppers! Mushrooms! And anchovies, and,"

"*And?* Do you know what you're getting yourself into? You might be making a monster!"

"That's fine," Sarah countered, rifling through a drawer of flyers and random papers. "I can handle it."

"If you say so," Mom warned with mock concern, washing her hands. "What do you say about a movie?"

"You, Mom, are a genius."

"You forgot patient, hardworking, b—"

"But,"

"But what?" Mom asked with a hand on her hip, interested and ignoring the interruption.

"Since I picked the pizza, you have to pick the movie."

"You sure?" Mom revealed a fiendish grin with perfect teeth. The child nodded. "Well, you're in for it now." A playful malice rang about her voice that gave Sarah the slightest pause, wondering what would be in store for her.

The kitchen was cleared of papers, folders and laptop, plates, napkins and glasses taking their place. Loud, meant-to-be-heard statements were made about how the living room was tidy, about who could have done such a good job.

Pillows and blankets were laid out for the movie, and a few games of twenty one questions were played while waiting for the pizza.

"So," Mom said, leaning forward, pursing her lips and looking up, thinking. "She's a fictional character, she doesn't die in the story, you're pretty sure she's married, she isn't a bad guy, and she was from a noble family."

"Right so far."

"Does she have magical powers?"

"Nope."

"Is she human?"

"Yup."

"Does she have magical armor?"

"Nope."

"Does she have a magical weapon?"

"Negative."

"Does she have a sword?"

"Mostly, yeah."

"Is she in a great battle?"

"Most definitely. That's eleven. Ten left," Sarah chided as she fought a yawn and stretched her arms across the table.

"Is she in—" Mom's twelfth question was cut short by her phone.

"Finally!" Sarah hopped down and sprinted to the door as Mom answered the call. Sarah opened the door to darkness and walked into it, hungry, hands out. The delivery man was a silhouette until Mom turned the lights on. He handed Sarah the box and looked at her mother. She stood sideways to sign the slip on the doorframe and for a moment Sarah was trapped between them and was staring at the pizza box, while the man's eyes moved over Mom. When she handed the slip back they shared a long, familiar smile. He waited a moment before folding the slip into his pocket and walking back to his car.

The pizza was too hot and delicious. "Wanna start the movie?" Mom asked, blowing on the tip of a slice.

"Nope, not yet."

Mom nodded and held up one finger. "Let's finish eating, because," then another finger, "it's so scary you'll choke on all that cheese." The challenge made Sarah plop her slice down and stare wide eyed, palms down on the table, wide set. Her eyes slimmed to daggers.

"Nine questions left," she challenged.

"Does she kill a person?"

Sarah picked up her slice and thought for a second. "Not a person, nope."

"Does she save someone's life?"

"Yeah," The child struggled through a bite too large. "Oh yeah."

"Multiple lives?"

She nodded.

"Is she a knight?"

Sarah thought long about this, finishing her first slice and grabbing a second, pulling it high so the cheese stretched and stretched before finally snapping.

"No."

"Does she have children?"

"No silly, she's probably not married." She offered with authority as she chewed.

"You don't have to be married to have kids," Mom corrected, finishing the crust of her first piece.

Sarah thought about this for a second. "Hm. Six more.

You're never gonna get it."

"Is she a champion of the people?"

"Yeah, I'd say so."

"Is she in Harry Potter?"

Sarah scoffed and shook her head. "Wasted that one."

"Is she an only child?"

"Nope! Dun dun dun…" she slowly raised her fingers in a menacing trident, reaching in for a third piece she knew she couldn't finish.

"Does she fall in love?"

Again Sarah brooded over this before revealing that yes, this unknown fighter did indeed fall in love.

"Is she," the back of the chair creaked with Mom's lean. "In *The Lord of the Rings*?"

Sarah's eyebrows perked and she nodded slowly.

"It's Arwyn!" Mom shouted, victory beaming from her face, a tenacity mimicked by her daughter's laughter.

"Nope! Hah!"

"Ah, you—what? Really? Then who is it?"

Sarah made her own chair creak and crossed her arms. "Never telling." Small shakes of her head and a wan smile was all she showed. "I'll give you a hint, though."

"Oh?"

"Yup. But," she said, leaning forward.

"There's always a but," Mom whispered through a smile. She tilted her head down and came to the table like her daughter.

Before making her offer, Sarah paused and almost balked, unsure how to exactly word her request. Mom was digging broccoli from her teeth when her daughter's words stopped her excavation. "Well, since Dad isn't coming home tonight," Sarah shifted her weight, played with her napkin. "I was wondering if it'd still be okay if I can go fishing tomorrow?"

"Fishing?" Mom looked up, eyebrows raised. "At that scummy lake way out back?" She snorted and clucked her teeth. "With all those bugs? Worms and hooks? Slimy fish? I mean, if you really want to, I guess."

The words rushed out of her. "I *promise* I won't touch the boat, I'll bring sunscreen, pack a lunch—"

"Boat?" Mom leaned back, hands on the edge of the table. She tapped a finger twice.

"It's only a twenty minute walk," Sarah lied. "And I'll have my phone with me."

"Yeah, sure honey," Mom said, getting up from the table with her phone in hand. "Just make sure you're careful with the, the uh," she held the phone to her ear.

"The hooks, yeah, I know," Sarah was beaming as Mom said to wait a minute, to clear off the table and wash her hands. Sarah swallowed a bite of her last piece, tossed it in the box and did as she was told, too excited to understand whispered words she wasn't allowed to say come from the other room.

As she was tucking the pizza in its bed Mom walked through the kitchen and into the living room without a word. The TV turned on and the volume was full blast, the explosion of sound jolted Sarah from her scrubbing and made Mom shout with a curse. It was on Sarah's channel, the cartoon was Kinshasa Kings, three shows after Carpet Mice. She tongued the cut in her mouth, waiting to be shouted at. Rustling blankets was all she heard so she finished cleaning the plate in her hands then hopped off the stepstool she hated, putting it under the cabinet and leaving a cup and some forks unwashed.

Blankets were unfolded, lights turned off, pillows adjusted, and they curled up beside each other waiting for the beginning credits to finish. Neither of them spoke. Something had happened, but Sarah didn't know what. She thought it was her fault until Mom started slowly braiding her hair.

"What did you pick?" Sarah asked with a yawn.

"It's an old one," she warned. "And scary."

"Those are always the best!" Sarah snuggled closer and slid further into the cushions as her eyelids grew heavy "What's it called?"

"The Blob."

"The Blob?" Sarah snorted. "What a silly name."

"Well, just wait and see."

Sarah's fight against the cousin of death was over twenty minutes into the film. Her mom sat awake, eyes trained on the screen but not watching the movie. The natural smell of her daughter, unwashed after a day of growth, always smelled like him. She tilted her head back and shifted side to side to get more comfortable.

The coffee table, the bookshelf, the mantle beneath the window, the case stocked with DVDs the television rested on.

They'd made all of it. Together.

She looked at the pictures that hung on the wall and barely saw them in the dim light, but not needing to, her memories of those days still fresh. She leaned back, continued to pet their daughter's hair, and sighed. A sudden urge to turn the movie off rushed through her, but instead she swallowed hard and wiped a tear from her cheek.

She bathed in but was not cleansed by the nostalgia of television light. With the infinite care granted only to mothers, she petted the long smooth hair of their sleeping cosmic union.

The stars bled into the night, sharing their distant light from the past, each of them dead or dying, awaiting their supernova fate as a lonely mother sat drowning in memories, wondering.

*　　*　　*

Sarah slammed awake from a bizarre dream she instantly forgot. The blankets were tucked around her with great care. A few minutes passed before she remembered the pizza, the movie, the chair.

The chair.

Slumping back down with the weight of embarrassment, the rest of the night filtered through her sleep fogged mind and she realized nothing was catastrophic, no one had died (*he was swallowed, swallowed and bones crushed to dust*), the only crime committed was not brushing her teeth. She sat and rolled the stiffness out of her neck, looking at the shapes of her familiar life through the pale blue light of early morning.

She held her hand up, the creases and knuckles strange in the odd hour. The thick silence that filled the world before it woke was exhilarating. Each moment pregnant with a million possibilities, her closed fist looking like an anvil upon which the future would be forged.

The world sparked into life with Sarah's preparations. Blankets folded, pillows stashed, extra clothes rolled and packed neatly next to a small first aid kit, poncho, hat, sun screen, multi-tool all put in their predetermined places, ready to be used. The pack was dropped by the door, hiking boots laced, bug-spray remembered and retrieved, all while the world dragged itself from the darkness and into graying day.

She scanned the open fridge and grabbed the half-gallon jug of milk and the pizza box at the same time, realized it wouldn't work, put the carton on the table first then returned for the box. Her half eaten piece was breakfast, and two more slices would be lunch. She jumped and pulled herself onto the counter and retrieved a tall glass and only after pouring too much milk did she realize she didn't want any at all. She stared at the glass with a frown. The liquid had a strange luminosity to it. She shrugged and put the carton and the box back home then walked over and pulled herself onto the counter next to the sink. She picked up a small glass from the mostly empty sink and rinsed it, then filled it with water and drank. She stopped after doing this twice more, the clear, cold water birthing gooseflesh along her thin arms, running a chill up her spine.

The window behind the sink provided a view of the trees she'd soon be trekking through. The gray sky seemed fractured by the topmost fingers of the trees. A parade of electric crowns reaching up and grasping nothing, the forest living in a strange torture of being rooted in the ground while struggling for the light above. Sitting on the counter, Sarah felt the first tendrils of hesitation creep through her like slow moving vines. The responsibility, the burden, the effort of what lay ahead shone in that unknowable darkness, and when a breeze rustled the tops of the trees she couldn't tell if it looked more like a greeting or a farewell.

Sarah burped. She giggled at the sound in the quiet kitchen, slid off the counter and walked to her pack. The second boot was almost tied when she stood abruptly and trotted back to the kitchen. She tripped on the untied laces and collapsed in a silent pile of youth and cotton. The boot was kicked off and the kitchen invaded by a twelve year old girl hopping on one foot, scrambling through a drawer of miscellaneous papers, knicknacks, markers and pens. She scribbled *GONE FISHIN! Be back later!* followed by a lopsided heart. She slid the note under a magnet with their family portrait on it.

Both boots secure, backpack on, adjusted, just right, Sarah walked out and shut the door with care before walking to the garage to get her pole and the tackle box.

The brown shed was the epitome of organization. Dad seemed to spend more time there than in the house. As she drew closer she remembered the heaps of wood that would be dragged in or would be spilling out of the open doors, and the sturdy pieces of furniture that would invariably be carried out. She'd helped paint and lacquer some of the pieces herself. But her favorite part was listening to her parents discuss the next piece, both of them poring over Mom's design and Dad discussing materials and tools. When Sarah heaved open the second of two doors she realized how long it'd been since the three of them had been inside together, and the emptiness that greeted her amidst these tools of creation dried her throat. She stood in the doorway a moment before entering.

The shed had an L-shaped workbench built into the walls which were covered by hanging tools color coded in a way that made perfect sense to Dad but looked now like a matrix of incomprehensibility. Three windows and the open door easily lit the entire room. A small chair and table sat in the far corner next to two dolls and their own tiny workbench. Sarah would pretend to build whatever Dad was, mimicking his left and right movements, sliding this way for a tape measure or to use the table saw, that way for nails or adhesives. She smiled and walked forward.

Her brand new pole was resting in a blue bag next to the tackle box. Her barely used, three month old birthday gift. Resting on the other side of the box was Dad's pole, disassembled but still as tall as her, the reel as big as both her fists, a deep green that always made her think of the ocean, even though she'd never been there. The pole leaned against the work bench she still couldn't see over. She reached down and shouldered the blue bag, then grabbed the handle of the gray and black tackle box and heaved. The instant the box was off the ground and in her control her father's pole listed to the left and its fall was imminent.

The clatter of the pieces hitting the packed-dirt floor was small and innocent but Sarah dropped the tackle box with a massive clunk and rushed to stand them up, almost stumbling head-first into the wall, catching herself just before she hit. She slowly picked them up and leaned them against the corner of the wall and the table, pausing a moment to ensure they wouldn't tumble down again.

After being certain they were safe, she adjusted her pole bag and grunted as she picked up the tackle box and walked out of the shed.

The path began at the back of the yard, the grass walked into oblivion by innumerable feet converging on a single span again and again. The transition of free, green life to never rebellious dirt was gradual but persistent, and Sarah was about to repeat what so many before her had done when she remembered. She sighed and slowly put down the tackle box and her pole. She walked back to the shed and leaned into each brown door, closing them. She thought about anything else she might have missed, then turned and skipped back to the path in the growing light. The path was still dark under its arched ceiling of trees.

Hibiscus dotted the ground on either side of her. Under the cover of trees, in the gloom of the young day, Sarah's entire world changed. She could taste the humid life thriving in every inch around her and the hum of open space was muted by the unquenchable aging of this new world she walked herself into.

The box grew heavy quickly and she switched hands regularly. The length of the walk she didn't remember exactly, but it wasn't terribly far, so she trekked on and began sweating with the pleasure of effort. Shadows were born and played around her feet as the sun rose, their slow games matched by the sounds of wind sifting through the branches. The ferns and bushes on either side of her invited her touch and caress, but she walked on, set to reach the lake. In a small clearing to her right, where the path didn't lead, a pool of sunlight revealed a wisteria tree waving to her in a tiny breeze, its light purple petals making her smile and feel at home in the rapidly aging day.

The struggle of that hooked fish flopping against her unstoppable strength and steady reel danced through her mind, its struggle immense but futile in the end.

Sweat beaded on her nose and forehead, her shoulder ached and her hands were raw, but she walked on, smiling in the silence. The park rangers who visited her school earlier in the week seemed a lot more interesting now that she could understand what it'd be like to be outside, in this, all day, your job to preserve and protect it. She pictured herself in the wide-brimmed hat, the green pants and pale green button up, giving advice to a family trying to start a campfire, shifting stones and clipping sapling branches to maintain a path, and when she imagined herself conducting a routine bird's nest count, she realized the silence that was upon her.

The birds and the wind had stopped. The shadows danced no more and the path grew darker. She finally began the long left turn that would bring her to the opening Dad had showed her. She squared her shoulders and stepped heavily, the thud of each foot reminding everything in the forest that she was there. With no breeze she began to sweat more, with no birds or whispers from the trees the only thing that seemed alive was her.

Dad told her to always throw the little ones back so they could grow to be big and fat, grow to become good enough to eat. She had a tingle at the base of her spine telling her that if some beast baited her into the water, she wouldn't be thrown back to land. A scene of her administering divine mercy on a tiny fish before engaging in a boxing match with some hulking tree-beast thousands of years old played through her head. After an exchange of blows that almost sent her reeling into the inescapable water, Sarah was finally victorious with a flying kick that she tried to mimic on the path, but instead stumbled, weighed down by her gear. She giggled to herself then rounded the corner and had all breath snatched from her lungs in a tremendous gust of terror.

The water was gone.

All of it.

The lake was still there, but instead of water it was filled with a viscous black pitch.

The tiny ripples and waves from the wind were replaced with an unnatural stillness reserved for the depths of nightmares and ancient, dry wells.

In the center was the green stem of an impossibly tall poppy flower with six red petals that seemed as wide as Sarah was tall.

Her feet inched her forward and the pain in her shoulder made her drop the tackle box and fishing pole. Her mind churned its young gears in futile attempts of comprehension.

Even the smell was gone. The musk of the wet soil was replaced by a confounding absence. Her inching stopped when she saw the boat, just as it should be, tied to the tree closest to the water, upside down and perfectly normal.

The silence and the bizarre abyss before the child sent her mind reeling and she felt like she was going to faint. She made small steps toward the boat, hands out. She was lost in that darkness, the only beacon being the stalk and the flower, and the point at which they joined, where it was neither and yet both at the same time.

Her hand was inches from the boat, from something real and remembered when there was a massive snapping sound as if the spine of the world was being ripped vertebrae from vertebrae. Sarah froze as the poppy jerked and a single petal fell and fell before finally hitting the liquid. It melted in a diseased swirl, the red defiant and bright but condensing to a single point, almost disappearing. Sarah stood and gawked as the crunching continued, the massive poppy lurching into the lake, the petals falling in turn.

She barely remembered to breathe. She shuffled her feet to the right, trying to get closer to the boat, to its peeling white paint and definite wood.

She huddled down on her haunches when the final petal fell and the stalk tumbled to its end. It caused no ripples. The liquid never moved. Not a splash, no evidence of the life and death of the once incredible poppy. What did remain was Sarah's terror and the swirling red of the melted petals which were congealing into six tiny beads. She was breathing hard and trying to rise when she heard the lake burp. It was quiet and far from the shore but unmistakable in the silence.

A lone ripple edged the line of unknown closer.

It stayed where it was, not receding.

Sarah held her breath, waiting.

A massive baritone belch made Sarah jump back and stumble over her feet. The ripple moved fast and crested into a small wave that sloshed on shore and landed on the bow of the boat with a heavy, wet slap. The edge of what used to be the lake didn't retreat. The liquid didn't drip from the boat, and the lake was again a picturesque stillness. Sarah's knees were locked as she stared at the spot on the boat where the liquid had touched the bow. It began to spread.

She tried to scream, but couldn't.

Her chest was heaving and sweat that had beaded began to fall from her face and her stomach turned in pain and disbelief as the boat was devoured by the unknown, the spot where she'd almost placed her hand now consumed.

A series of shrieks erupted from the center of the lake, each making their own waves that consumed more and more soil, more and more of the boat. Their familiarity anchored Sarah and their tone terrified her. She was a bundle of infantile whimpers.

A huge surge of liquid headed by three pairs of red eyes raced towards her. She crawled backwards, eyes wide and wrists weak. Her elbow hit the tackle box and she screamed, releasing her own immense claim to existence, only to be met by more animal-like shrieks and more consumptive pitch.

Sarah scrambled to her feet and heard a third series of shrieks and an otherworldly, wet tear. She stared and thought herself in a dream or some other transitory state as three horse heads were born into her world. They tore through the surface and rushed towards her. The bag with her fishing pole tangled her feet and she fell again. The horses fought each other for freedom from some cracked obsidian omphalos, together moving forward, each impossibly huge and scrambling on top of the liquid like newborn demons. Their muscles were rippling and their reins were thick.

The child thought it all fake, all some unreal film flashing before her eyes until the violent clopping of the hooves shot out and echoed back again. She clapped her hands over her ears and squinted in pain. The three were almost finished birthing themselves when another shriek pierced her hands and forced life into her knees.

She ran.

She pumped her limbs through shadows that no longer danced but leered and mocked her short legs. The horses were loud and furious and sprinting, raging across the lake and bearing down on the land, frothing and chasing after her, spitting their oblivion every which way, their reins carrying no carriage but tethered to some charge untold fathoms below the surface. Once touched she would be consumed, just like the boat and the leaves and trees.

The bend was longer than she remembered. For a second she thought about the pole and the tackle box and how they were lost forever. The path was wider and her legs were already burning. The world opened and expanded with each step and her gasps for air were lost in the sheer vastness of it all. The horses with their unfathomable yoke raced ahead, closing the distance between the free youth and the tethered beasts. She ran, but the fact of their speed and size was undeniable.

The turn ended and in senseless childhood curiosity her head turned.

She saw nothing to match the rhythmic clatter that resonated through the forest and her bones. Her legs slowed, she turned to trot backwards. Lying to herself, she conjured a thought of safety, knowing full well she was about to face all the terror that nature had born.

The obsidian horses with eyes like the sun rounded the corner and they carried with them the end of everything the child knew. The forest behind the horses wilted and was consumed by their spit and urine as it splashed everywhere. They were tethered to a darkness, an all consuming wall Sarah could not look away from, one about to devour her and all the open space behind her. The child tried to run but tripped over herself. The trio galloped forth like the unstoppable movement of night to day. The ground, the trees, her mind shook with their approach and she knew she would succumb. As they thundered forward acceptance rushed through her in one calm breeze. This is how it happens. She would become one with the unknown, bound to whatever fate was inscribed for her in the depths of her future. Her eyes closed and she waited, knowing the change to be seconds away, the roar tremendous and bearing down.

Their charge continued. Their presence was feet away when the world was shocked to stillness. The only sound was her haggard breathing. Her eyes were shut tight but she could sense their shapes nonetheless. The child stood with clenched fists before the dripping horses.

She opened her eyes.

They were tall and terrible. Their eyes red with the poppy petals, flaming and churning orbs of crimson, their bodies perfectly still. They weren't breathing. A faint mist rose from their bodies. They bristled as Sarah's eyes moved over their reins and bit collars. They seemed to glisten with faint and scattered grains of light. When she noticed the mist seeping from where the restraints touched their bodies, she inhaled and the horses reared up and shrieked. The child jumped back but wasn't scared and as their charge pulled their reins tight the horses toppled over backwards, splashing into the eternal stillness. Sarah felt the world dilate around her. She became a mote of pollen in the forest.

A vast presence was approaching. Something unstoppable, like the fall from a high tree after a snapped branch or failed grip.

She hooked her thumbs underneath the straps of her backpack and pulled it off. Without her bag she felt light and free, almost as if she could float up and through the ceiling of nothingness that bisected her world, through to something pure and carefree.

But that dilation, the expansion of everything around her, continued and with it a foundation of dread in the pit of her stomach, nurtured by some brazen bricklayer.

The child stood on the cusp between worlds. And then she saw the hand.

It pressed out but was held back by the black surface, pushing but unable to break the tension, unable bring whatever it was into being. The fingers stretched the pitch then receded. A second hand appeared and the being thrust itself forward, wanting desperately to be born, to break free from whatever world it inhabited, past or future. Two fingers pierced through and Sarah felt something in her break. A hand and elbow slowly pushed through the opening. Then another hand broke free.

The slender arms were a different obsidian than the horses. They were iridescent, alive with tiny flecks of light, a living night sky, and somehow familiar. The arms, once through, ceased moving and were held high. A head squeezed through and Sarah could see it was a woman.

With a sigh the woman was born and continued lifting herself, somehow, from the nothingness into the forest. The contours of her face were perfect and made visible by cobalt shadows and glacial veins. The light from Sarah's brown and green world played on this being's skin like the symphony of colors that erupts when oil meets water. Her shoulders were out and when Sarah saw the curves of her breasts exposed an unrecognizable feeling swam through her and she wanted to look away but couldn't. Sarah again felt that uncanny familiarity, and it mingled with her fear. The being continued to birth itself, the shapely ribs, flat stomach, blooming hips and a triangle of pubic hair alive with a thousand prismatic colors, all lifting from the farthest places of our sanity.

The thighs and knees revealed themselves in complete silence. The instant her toes were exposed the creature opened its eyes and mouth, revealing opaline eyes and teeth, luminescent and beautiful in their horror. The first step was soundless until leaves crunched underfoot. Her touch spread nothing of the void she came from. With another step she opened her arms in a welcoming embrace. She made a sound that was either sardonic laugh or casual growl.

Neither of them moved. The child waited with sweaty palms and a dry mouth.

"Who are you?" Her voice was tiny before the being.

"I'm who you're going to be." Her voice was a hive of wasps.

Sarah took a step back. "You can't be." She wanted to stand tall and confront this claim, but the creature sensed her fear and grew with it. Soon it stood taller than her parents. "I'm not scared of you," the child lied, taking two more steps.

"You don't have to be," the winged insects hummed louder. "Yet." The syllable of violence buzzed from its throat as it took a step forward, covering the distance of Sarah's three strides. "Do you know what I am?"

Sarah was silent. Its teeth were bigger than Sarah's fingers and its skin was roiling in supernovas.

"I," it began as a wasp crawled from its mouth, walked across the face and into an ear. "Am all the injustice you shall bear, all the contempt you shall reek," its hips turned with the birth of another step. "All the lies and despair you shall wade through," it leaned forward and its breasts hung in front of Sarah's eyes. They looked at each other, face to face.

"I am all the evil you will endure," a trio of wasps came from her nose, one flying away, the other two finding her mouth. Her eyes were massive and opaque, shifting as if a million wings fluttered inside them. "For being beautiful." The final word was a sigh that released a dozen wasps, all crawling in and out of her face. The woods burst alive with their agitated buzzing.

The creature massive and bent so, Sarah was close enough to touch it. She continued to take clumsy steps backward as the trees moved with a growing breeze, their rustle harmonizing with the buzzing. The creature's eyes fluttered madly with the terrible truth that lived inside and when Sarah shook her head and took another step, it began to inhale a breath so great Sarah's hair began flying towards it. The breath was impossibly long and as its back and chest swelled all trunks and branches bent in towards it.

As a gust for a moment dampens a fire before igniting it, the creature drew in breath. The creaking of its jaws was a cavalcade of snapping roots. Its eyes burned a radiant white. Its mouth stretched wide, wider, wide enough to swallow the child whole.

It belched a swarm of wasps and the child ran.

The trees, released, sang overhead. The wasps sounded electric behind her and the guttural bellow from the beast shook the ground. She ran as fast as her small legs would take her, through the chaos that surrounded her and away from the impending unknown. The creature spoke, but Sarah couldn't understand the words, blood pounding in her ears, legs burning, the swarm close enough to feel the collective beating of their wings. Sweat dripped down her face and back, her legs covering only inches with each stride, panic rising in her chest.

She wouldn't make it. She was too short, too weak to outrun the swarm.

But there it was—the end of the path, the trees ending, the lush grass waiting, her house just beyond.

Pain bloomed in her lower back but she kept running, scratching at and killing a wasp, wiping its innards on the back of her thigh. She tossed the carcass to the ground.

The swarm was almost upon her. She was feet from the door. The creature bellowed one last time and the sound rolled deep in Sarah's guts. The door was opened and slammed in an instant, the few wasps in uncared for and millions more crashing and piling into each other, their chaos drowned by sobs from the only child.

Her mom rushed in and dropped her phone, cradling her child who lay on her side, slick with tears and sweat and terror. She knelt and propped Sarah on her lap, issuing senseless but soothing words. A kiss was planted on her forehead and more calm words spoken before her breathing slowed.

The child could smell the coffee and cigarettes on her mother's breath. Sarah opened her eyes and saw her mother's face then kicked away from her, screaming, slamming into the leg of the kitchen table.

Her mother's eyes were gone.

Replaced by the fluttering opaline discs of the beast. Gushing from her mouth were uncountable wasps. Sarah screamed and there was an explosion of glass beside her. A thin layer of milk spread across the brown tiled floor, the white sheen growing thinner and thinner until it almost wasn't there anymore.

"Sarah!"

The wasps were gone.

Her mother's eyes were rimmed with fear and care and tears. Sarah leaned towards her mother but she was just out of reach and her hand landed in a piece of glass. She gasped and drew back as a few drops of blood fell into the milk. The mother hugged the child until the sobbing stopped, clutching the child's palm to stop the bleeding.

Sarah's eyes never left the door.

Her mom saw her staring. She wiped the child's face with a palm and grunted as she picked her daughter up to carry her to the kitchen sink.

The milk was cleaned and Sarah, in a blanket, was cocooned on the couch, bleeding into a bandage.

Her mother opened the door and stared out into the shadows between the trees. She crossed her arms after a minute and closed the door.

*   *   *

Her father closed the shed doors and headed for the path with deliberate strides, carrying him in loping, repeating S-curves. His eyes were trained on the ground. The treetops swayed every which way under the gray sky. The breeze was cool and it raised gooseflesh on his arms as he came into the shade of the trees. His breathing was deep and loud in the silence, and for a moment, the life that surrounded him pressed a cosmic loneliness into his bones with enough force to slow his gait to a stroll.

The vastness of the forest when his family first moved here seemed diminished somewhat. He saw instead the grass that fed the beetle, that in turn fed the robin, that in turn fed the hawk. Not a marvellous collection of life, but an orderly system of predation.

His lazy curves continued, his eyes wandering about, wondering what had caused his daughter so much grief. The clearing with the wisteria tree was littered with its lavender petals, the tree's branches half exposed. Forest air filled his lungs as a breeze peeled off a flurry of petals that scattered about randomly.

He trained his eyes upward at the first or second branches of the largest trees, looking for a nest. His foot hit something large and he almost fell, but he just stumbled and cursed before regaining his balance. It was Sarah's backpack. He shook his head and shouldered it onto his back, loosening the straps.

Halfway around the corner and the breeze of the lake flirted with the hairs on his arms and he breathed deep, looking around and walking slow. The rustle of the small waves and the sight of the abandoned tackle box, tipped but closed, and Sarah's pole, still zipped with a bit of dirt and what looked like sap on it, made him smile. Sarah's dad stood at the edge of the lake and stared out. He let the water lap at his feet for a few minutes. The boat was still moored as he'd left it, the peeling white paint reminding him of the patch on Sarah's ceiling he needed to fix.

After another long gaze across the water, at the ripples and the shadows, he hooked his thumbs through the straps of his daughter's backpack and turned around. The walk felt further than it did the first time, probably because of Sarah's gear. A slow pride bloomed in him as he thought about how she carried all of the gear out this far, preparing everything as she did so, and doing it by herself.

He stepped on something with a distinct, hollow crunch. He tilted his shoe to the side and saw the yellow and black husk of a crushed wasp.

The Desert and the Sea

For miles in every direction, there's only desert. The path of her footsteps is long and undisturbed, dimples and curls on the orange sand like faded lines of cursive script. She says in a throat of bristles and grit, "I cannot go back."

She stands at the peak of a sand dune and sees the crooked spine of a thousand more dabbled upon the earth by some mammoth painter. Licking cracked lips with a tongue of clay she says, "I'm not thirsty."

She continues down the shapeless dune, her feet slapping and sliding ever faster with the slope. Her speed is of no concern to her aching feet, creaking knees or screaming hips. Her body trembles with each step, the dune carelessly marking her progress. *If I ignore it,* she thinks, *the pain will disappear, as the ocean carries away sand and pebbles to build beaches worlds away.*

She reaches the bottom of the dune and is about to start up the next when a tsunami of memory brings back the statues of her past. Built near the sea, they are amazing creations of precision and beauty, crafted as tall, permanent statements with the familiar faces of friends and family. She looks behind at her footsteps and perceives a misplaced beauty in the trail of half-moon swirls and decides, incorrectly, that it's just too far back, that she simply can't. She wants no monument, and so turns to the next dune as a small breeze begins filling the dimples in the sand.

A breath of wind almost knocks her down: her healthy curves were devoured by her journey. Now she is a brittle tree without leaves being toppled by that tiny breeze. "I'm not hungry," she mutters to herself, thinking she says it with a

Ignorance is the easiest answer to every question

smile.

Trying to take a step, she slumps down and a few grains of red sand cover the tips of her fingers. The breeze continues, pushing it up to her wrists. *This is what I want*, she tells herself as she digs her fingernails in, her mind awash in the monuments of her past.

The breeze is small but it does not quit. Soon her ankles are gone and the red sand is climbing up her knees. Shapeless slopes are forming around her.

She knows, somewhere, that she can move, shake the sands of imagined inevitability from her body and follow what's left of her footsteps back to the smell of sea salt. But the weight of senseless shame has anchored her and she takes senseless pride in her own passive burial.

She thinks of the statues: defined, polished, cut with intent and chiseled with care. She thinks of the never still, thundering, blue and white waves.

The patient red sand continues to inch its way up, devouring her body with its formless appetite, the border of the inevitable now around her neck. She has chosen to surround herself with shapeless dunes. Her footsteps barely remain as the rising sand passes her eyes. The final strands of her hair twitch in the breeze like exposed roots.

Her dune builds and builds and with time she becomes just another stroke on the canvas of the mammoth painter.

As the Wind Is

Wind gives life to grass, bushes
to the fingers of trees
it spreads seeds, swoops sundresses
and undresses the sun.
The composer of migrations
mighty waves and rainy days.

There are viscous vines
clinging, in the depths of a dry well.
They are the apathy of the unable to eat
The questions with no answers
The old with no wisdom
The young with no lust.
They are as the wind is,

as love is a knife
or hatred a gift.
Wind is endless
as the vines are not.

Within the well
are threads of a rope.
So spin, twist, braid,
and be as the wind is:
never still.

The Climb

Shadows, those cousins of the sun, invite
an adventure—the tree is found.
A grasshopper springs, away.
Wide at the base, a blooming crown
of leaves racing from the ground,
scared of the sky.
The lowest branch asks first.

Bark sings against palms.
The answer is slow and deliberate. A moment
of sitting, looking up, before
a cavalcade of questions
rains down from above.
After the first branch, the climb is rapid.

The next branch presents itself
and leads to the following, then another.
Soon a search is needed before each climb.
Here, a look reveals the ubiquity of the simple grass below,
the delicate thinness of branches this high.

A gaze raised, a slow stance,
cocked knees and a leap to the highest
which never is
—from the street a cataclysmic roar of collision—
a grasp but no grip, and the tumble begins.

Branches snap, slap and crush
bruising and bleeding the adventurous,
until the lowest and oldest branches catch.

Scale the Sycamore

The grass is not greeted.

The path of the fall is seen,
as are the highest branches.
The climb begins anew.

Racing through known melodies
deaf to the cries in the flame, hearing only

the cousins' call for light.

Eat the Sycamore, Drink the Sea

We are all born in blood, but
the days of swimming in death
are dead themselves.

War, pathogen, stupidity nor weakness kill us.
Now, the double sided axe
of gluttony and civilization

Hews away our perception of that terminal vastness.
The sap of our lives dribbles away
along with the atomic beauty within.

Our roots decay unseen
as our crown is devoured
for a batch of newspapers.

we all felt the nausea

we all heard the roar
we all chose, chose to be deaf

Second Shift

and get drunk on our own destruction

With only seeing the blood and not the gunshot wound itself, I know Kevin won't keep the leg. Cameron's careful to not wrench the case from his hands, and takes it slowly with a gentle nod and sad eyes. We drag Kevin onto the table. He's twitching and rubbing the palms of his hands into his eyes. He mutters obscenities and jibberish. Bianca and Robert peel off their flour laden latex gloves for fresh ones, soon to be covered in our friend's blood.

Cameron gauges the weight of the case without opening it and builds her own story of the pops outside without asking for my version.

"Were you followed?"

"For a bit. Bordwells usually roll pretty deep, but we lost them in the yards. We gotta send someone around to put the chains back on, and clean up the—" I point my thumb behind me and shake my head.

Cameron nods, hands me the case, puts a hand on her belly and grimaces. Before exiting through the door Kevin and I entered, she pours me a whiskey. I let the first mouthful sit and fight against the cotton, anxiety, and fear in my mouth. I empty the glass with three swallows into relief, safety, and the next step.

Bianca and Robert carry Kevin from the door and onto a table they'd cleared of measuring cups and sifters. They cut his left pant leg open, exposing what's left of his knee. He can't look at it and I can't look away. Bianca places a hard plastic tube in his mouth. He bites, blinks quickly, and I want to tell him it'll be okay when Cameron returns. "That'll be okay for the night, but that has to be cleaned before sunrise.

How far away were you?"

"Point blank," handing her the cup. She nods with inwardly pursed lips, and we share a moment's silence.

"How much did you lose?"

"Half."

She shakes her head and sighs. "If we lose any more we'll be making crackers instead of bread."

"Tonight was sloppy. We need to figure out something for these new guys. The guy who tapped Kevin tried to lift the case, he thought it was *coke*. I—"

"I know. Things are—" she puts her hands on her knees and inhales sharply before walking to the bathroom.

"We think the State's bribing again," she continues through the door. "Or at least using air strikes and roadblocks to squeeze out intel. We barely have enough juice to keep our lights on and ovens hot, but they've got flocks of drones so we haven't been able to get our own eyes up."

I bite my lower lip and try to not think about the big picture. I pull the Bluetooth from my ear and put it next to a moldering collection of Isaac Asimov short stories. I plug it in out of habit, getting no charge. "When will we be ready to move?"

She opens the door. "That's not on us this time. One of the refrigerators on Plantation Street went to shit—" muted screams, soothing words, and two professionals continuing their conversation, "—so the next stop is low on butter. They don't want to split shipments, so we're going to hold the rest here until it's solidified again."

I stand and make my way to the door while rolling my shoulders backward, relishing the soreness and the rub of my holsters under each arm. I flex my wrists and fingers trying to wring the vibrating steering wheel from them.

"Where're you headed?" Cameron asks.

"Gotta clean up my little mess out back."

"Save that for those two," Cameron says, nodding her head at Robert and Bianca. "There's still work to do."

We walk upstairs and the door clicks shut behind us as

the grunts and muffled screams crescendo. I follow Cameron into the kitchen and begin disassembling my left pistol as she takes out a large box from beneath the sink and three smaller sized ones from cabinets on either side. Her pistols are on the table, disassembled for cleaning. "We're on protection tonight, running guns for the Racks. They're moving some essentials to the Dozers," she says. "Soap, disinfectant, water and air filters." I finish laying out all the parts. "Syringes, gloves. Probably some batteries."

I pause and fish my tongue around my teeth. Two scars on my right arm burn in remembered pain. "Where to?" I ask, straightening my back and scrubbing the barrel.

"Across the river." Cameron's assembling her own gear, checking magazines, counting grenades.

"Oh," I say involuntarily, relieved at the fact we can take the—

"No boats, though."

"What? Why?"

"Too much noise, they said."

I pause and look up to meet her eyes. "We haven't taken the bridge in almost a year, not since the partitions."

"Yup."

"Is the checkpoint on the west side still up?"

"We think so."

I sigh and put both palms on the table, look down and clear imagined food from my teeth. There are certain questions I have to ask, but as a friend, a victim, and a soldier, those are questions I don't want to. Cameron gives me the answers anyway.

"We'll have help. Based on Burc's last drone runs two weeks ago, the infrastructure of the checkpoint is still there but it isn't heavily manned. Two, four guards tops. No running and gunning this time, so I'm told. We're there just in case. We'll talk tactics with the Racks down by the old school."

I continue cleaning my pistols.

Things are changing. The ebb and flow of old politicking had largely vanished when the national checkpoints were established, but now cogs were turning and pieces moving. People were beginning to realize which bolts were important, who was greasing what, and who were simply bells and whistles.

We occupy our silence with velcro rips and rounds snapping into place. The tumult below tells us we are losing another good man of action to the permanent silence of death or the stillness of paralysis.

After double checking each other's gear and sharing half of a brown apple, Cameron moves to the door. I inhale, not sure of what I'm going to say and she looks back.

"Burc says we won't have to worry about our shipments anymore. He said—he said we'd be able to just work. No more shit like tonight. He knows what we're into, and he knows how things have been lately. People've been talking about something big, not a full on treaty or a truce, but something, at least. Nobody wants—"

"How the fuck is he going to promise some shit like that? He *doesn't* know what things are like, he's holed up and has his game locked down, he's safe and sound and basically untouchable. He has his people who run for him, we're the ones—"

"Nobody wants to see people dying just to live," she barks back, pointing at the door leading downstairs. "We aren't superheroes, we're surv—we're fighters." I clench my fists and take a long, slow breath. She puts both hands on my elbows. "He says he's got something. What do we got?"

I look around. Everything is in it's place and falling apart, rot from inside, neglect from outside. A clock that doesn't tick, books with burnt pages, windows that refuse light and faded pictures of a family none of us know. I nod slowly and speak quietly. "We've been in for less than an hour, the Bordwells are still roaming—"

"If we take my bike, they won't be a problem."

Screams from the basement are choked off by friendly hands. The shock of her words hit me like the bullet did him, but where pain diluted his mind, questions mire mine. *Safe passage? Who paid who off? With what? Why only you?*

Cameron sighed. "Everything—" she shook her head in genuine confusion, "—it's turning into a clusterfuck. Weird to say it, but two years ago things were a lot more simple." I see her eyes looking for answers. "Look at it like this. We're not carrying any goods. If it gets too hot, we're out. We do this run, and we have safe passage from the Bordwells and everyone else. This is a one-time contract gig." I see something else in her eyes. "I'm not dying for them."

I snort back a laugh. The daily reminders of the fragility of life turn me somber or grateful, apathetic or fiery, but only the unpredictability of human decision confuses me.

We hop on a motorcycle with two different sized wheels, only the left rear view mirror, a broken speedometer and a smell that brings out the chiding mechanic in me.

She kicks the engine into life.

Our ride is silent. The deep blue moonlight bathes everything and is a welcome curtain for the daylight that shows only how close to death everything is. I pull apart the last few hours to see what I could have done safer, better, faster. The droning blue is erased by gunshots and screams from behind me, a gurgling noise that only means a bullet to the neck and I clear my throat to bring myself back onto the bike.

I swallow and want a drink. I see a small fire ahead and reach for a pistol on Cameron's left hip but she shakes her head before turning it. "Just a bum, throwing the only answer up." I squint and see the single index finger raised high, stretching for the useless stars.

I relax my arm and see Kevin's smirk after I evaporated the man's face who held a gun to his own. Kevin was good. He was a professional. Now? Now, at best he's just a cripple, at worst he's another trip to the burning fields—

"*Shit!*" a handful of pops as we pass by the fire, I reach for her right pistol but as I turn backward to return a few rounds Cam swerves left and right, sending my shots wild. "Hit?" she asks.

Mental check. "Nope."

"Bike?"

Physical check. "Nope."

"Motherfucker," she hisses. "Who the fuck does that?"

"It's a clusterfuck, remember?" I chuckle as I replace her pistol.

"Yeah, but—" she shakes her head and sighs, lowers her shoulders and accelerates.

The monochrome jungle is alive. So am I. But for how long? Goosebumps race along my arms as I remember something Burc said a few months back: predators don't dwell in the past.

We drive about three miles from my screaming friend and we're about three more from the river when we pull into the Racks' station. An abandoned school for the deaf four stories tall and next to a fire station. Both are brick monoliths amongst rotting or burned wood houses and shops. When the temperatures rose, the polluted humidity seeped into everything and began eating it from the inside out, devouring buildings, plants, and people.

Eight or nine people are out front. Masks, leather gloves, pipes, nailed baseball bats, chains. One of them has an AK, most of them have pistols under their arms or on their hips. Who knows what gadgets they have rigged up and down the block. Half the lights are on in the building and the door to the garage is wide open. A pair of halogen lamps cast grotesque shadows and make me squint. They're expecting us, so they part and let us ride through a sliding, layered chain link fence that used to be the front door.

From the fence and the squad outside, the Racks seemed to be gearing up to compete with the Bordwells. That was odd, because they don't have to. They have Mike de Burca. Former Assistant to the Head of the Public Works Department, he knows the bones and blood of the Greater Boston area like a chef does his kitchen. He's the most valuable man for a hundred miles in any direction.

The tops of desks are boarded together and nailed to the first seven or eight doors we walk past. The legs of the desks are laced together and tied with thin ropes. Every seven or eight paces there's about three feet of slack. Cameron sees me looking and she explains how these are used defensively, like pike warfare. Pull the slack, the legs shoot up at an angle, no one gets in. If they try, they're stuck, and soon dead.

We pass a mural of flowers in the main foyer, and I see Kevin's erupted knee in a patch of roses. I blink and look away, still seeing it. "I gotta chat with Burc. We'll go over tactics in about twenty," she says with a nod toward a door. I turn the knob and welcome the solitude.

A single fluorescent bulb, gray walls, no windows, a long tattered couch that used to be green, a white round table with three chairs around it. I choose the couch, close my eyes and tilt my head back.

I feel the shaking take root in my wrists and my fists tighten. I breath in deep through my nose and out my mouth. Three counts of three: in, hold, out. In, hold, out. In, hold, out. The smell of Cam's bike has soaked into my clothes, and I—

—finally released the clutch a full ten seconds after I killed the engine. She still hadn't opened the door and didn't seem to be doing much aside from waiting. I started to sweat. My handlebars were my only friends and I wasn't about to let them go.

She got out and began the deliberate saunter. She was miles away and the journey from her white cruiser to my black bike took years. She reached her destination and pivoted, waiting for me to remove my helmet. I carefully obliged.

"License," she said, giving my bike a slow once over before stabbing my eyes with her own. "And registration."

My helmet was in my lap and my face was stone. "It's in my bag. May I?"

"By all means." She motioned with her right arm before resting it on the butt of her pistol. She followed me the two steps back and put a half pace more between herself and the bike. That was important. That allowed me to breathe.

"My bag's locked in here," I tapped one of the two red metal boxes strapped above my rear wheel. She waited, silent.

I reached for the keys in the ignition. I thought of the joke about how Ronley sneezed in front of a cop and got three in the chest. This time it wasn't very funny.

I didn't know how many trips the boxes had made, but it was definitely more than I had.

"Officer—" she raised her eyebrows, "full disclosure." Her face was still but her body smiled. "There's an open container of alcohol inside. But —"

"It's locked, I know."

"Would you do the honors, then?" I held the keys out. "Just so you can verify it's actually locked."

She pursed her lips and shook her head. "Liability. Wouldn't want to be responsible for damaging such—" she thumbed at one of the dozens of craters in the metal, "precious cargo."

I nodded. I popped the lock and she walked around, keeping her distance, peeking inside. The gallon jug of Crown Royal was all she looked at as I ruffled through papers, tools, and a dog-eared copy of *House of Leaves*.

I handed her my license and registration and she stuffed them in her pocket without looking. "Step in front of the vehicle." I looked at her. I took a breath and she ordered: "There. Now." She pointed to the opposite side of the bike. I obliged. She picked up the bottle and admired it as a mother would a newborn daughter.

"Contraband." She wiped her thumb over the PURE CANADIAN engraved in the glass. "Imported liquor was banned almost a year ago." I knew this, but put my face in my hands and was about to start reciting the script we were taught when: "Open the other one."

She uncorked the bottle, hooked index and thumb around the handle, put her other forearm underneath the bottle and tipped it to her mouth. Her following sigh was disgusting and infuriating.

"Now."

I started to move then stopped, and the hesitation unlocked the clasp on her pistol. "I—"

"Am going to open it. *Now.*"

"— need the key."

She snorted and sipped quickly, stepping back and motioning me forward.

I walked, heel toe, heel toe, over to the opened box and removed the key. I turned my back to her and returned to the other side. She walked in lockstep with me, the whisky jostled, happy to be used.

The key slid in. She took a step forward as I opened the box to reveal dozens of sealed glass jars filled with beige pellets. "Is that—?" an eyebrow cocked.

She drops the jug and it shatters, the liquor drank by the garbage in the gutter. I launch a kick at her right wrist but it lands high, in the elbow, she grabs my ankle and pulls. I'm off balance and catch a fist in the neck. I hit hard with a left to her chest and as she staggers, I kick off the ground. We fall together, my legs straddling her, and I bring both fists down on either side of her neck. She blocks and jabs my lips with both arms. I taste blood as she twists her hips and flips me. As she kneels over me her head bumps harmlessly off the red container and I land a solid left between her nose and top lip and get a grip on her throat with my right.

Her barbaric choke for air is horrible and satisfying.

She falls to her left and her arm moves for her pistol but I'm on top and lock her elbows with my knees.

Her face is burgundy and the panic spasms start.

I grip harder and look into her eyes—I see her begging and helpless *and about to die* and I can't stop. I grind my knees and squeeze and squeeze and squeeze. Her eyes are begging, blue is seeping into her skin, her eyes are red and wide and begging and begging but my hands can't stop and I feel something shift and crumble in her throat. She starts shaking, her legs flailing, weak and slowing down, her face swollen and purple.

I stood and looked at the broken glass we'd almost rolled in and kick her before vomiting. Some of it splashed onto her face and I coughed out half a sob. I stepped backwards into the middle of the street and looked at what I'd done. I don't know how long I stood there but I checked to make sure the yeast was fine and locked both boxes after taking her pistol, ammunition, mace, taser, her ID, my fake papers, and checking for a dashboard cam. We knew their hand radios didn't work anymore, so I used her binoculars to check for traffic both ways before siphoning off her gas.

I put my helmet on and the key home. The engine roared freedom and food for at least a few. "What a waste of good—"

"—whiskey?" I jerk forward and my chin hits a glass in front of my face, splashing a bit on my lips. The slow fire is delicious. I look at him, at the glass, back at him and he shrugs. "It's watered down, but not bad." He waits and I take the glass. He sits on the far end of the couch.

"Thanks." I wipe the memory from my eyes, my heart pounding. I go to take a sip, stop, then extend to the right and wait for the accompanying *clink*. "Stephan."

"Riley."

My first sip is tasteless and I eventually swallow. I turn and look him. "Sorry, didn't catch that."

He looks over. "Riley. Like smiley," he says, pasting a goofy grin and poking a cheek with a finger. Even though it's fake, the smile makes the wrinkles on his face disappear. If it wasn't for the pale blue rash creeping up his neck and into his scalp he would look ten years younger. We drink for a moment in silence.

"You come in with Cam?"

I nod and savor the warmth spreading in my throat and belly.

"Hm," he responds, swirling his drink. He wants to ask a question but doesn't know how, so I watch his eyes follow the swirls of ice in his whiskey, the delicacy slowly melting and becoming nothing.

We both sip and wait.

"You always been in protection?"

The question escapes me and I ask him to repeat it.

"Protection? No, I've been—"

"Fuckin typical," he mumbles and leans back. I lean forward, eyebrows cocked, half wishing my pistols were too. "Sorry—it, it's nothing with you, man." He sighs and slumps down. He shakes his head slowly. "It's just," he coughs, "we never used to do stuff like this. I mean, think about it. Farmers farm. Teachers teach. Cooks cook. We don't do shit like this. We run info. I mean, sometimes we sabotage when our lanes get clogged, but that's it. We're not built for this stuff, let alone stuff this big."

I tilt my cup, raise my eyebrows and shake my head.

"I don't know details, but our run tonight is to the Dozers. Shelise and Brandon are talking like it's our last one." *The Racks not running info anymore? Who's on news, then? What game were they getting into now?* "They're saying the order tonight is for the Dozer's girls, and we'll be snagging up some artillery and quick charge battery systems."

"What artillery?"

"I've heard it all the past few days, but mostly car crushers, cluster napalm charges and rail gun we can fuck around with and get mounted on our largest bird."

I take a sip and think. His alcohol speaks for him.

"We've started boobytrapping State supply lines in the sewers the past two months, I'm not sure why we're moving into such, I dunno," he pauses, looking for the right words. "Such openly aggressive stuff. We used to just run mostly two man jobs, nothing big, no cavalry. Blast charges under manholes, weaken key roads, slow burn corrosives on their water mains. But, shit, now, if we're really grabbing this stuff, with this many people…" he trails off and finishes his drink.

He carries an ancient and beautiful .357 under his arm. On his hip is a .380 Smith and Wesson Bodyguard, a clunky, greasy, impressive gun.

Eleven shots. Must be how many he's taken, too.

My shortness of breath and tense wrists remind me to take my pills. I wash two of them down with the rest of the whiskey, but one of them gets caught. I cough it up and bite down. The crunch brings me back to the cop's throat.

He snorts, smirks, "Last week, we—"

The door opens, it's Cam. "We're out in 30." She looks at the glass in my hand.

We're walking down a hallway and I'm trying to ignore the roses on the mural and keep my stomach calm. "What are we up to tonight, boss?"

"We'll debrief with Burc and his crew then roll out." *I thought she already talked with him?*

"What time will we get home tonight?"

"This is a one and done. We run them through the checkpoint, make sure they get to the Dozers, then we head back. All in all, two hours, maybe three. We're more than welcome to kill some time at the Dozers, I've heard." She smiles and I see where her mind is going, but I need to stay focused.

"Then why the briefing?" Our footsteps echo.

"Burc's cooking something up."

"I'm not sure if I'm that hungry. We have other people to feed—" She raises her hand and shakes her head to stop me. I hear a voice through a door at the end of the hallway.

She stands in front of the door, looking me in the face. The skin around her eyes is traced in shallow wrinkles. Bags rest beneath them like ash around embers. If she wasn't my best friend, my boss, a killer, I would have kissed her, even with Riley standing there. She speaks slowly. "We know why we're fighting. They do too. Different reasons don't mean different goals. Besides, there's a light at the end of our tunnel."

She smiles and flicks her tongue out, doesn't wait for my response, then turns the knob and leans into the door. Burc's voice wafts over me and he doesn't skip a beat in his speech. There's twelve or thirteen people, most sitting, all silent, staring at a bald, bearded collection of bones and scars in the front of the room. Behind him is a map on a dirty monitor with symbols and dotted lines decorating a small segment of the Charles River. I look at the map, hearing the sound of his voice but not listening to the words, and I think about our lives: local, roughshod, barely understandable.

"...this fight is bigger than us." He speaks with slow care. "I may not know where you were all born, but I know where you're from." He breathes loudly, wheezing a bit. "This petty shit—this family on family street politics, who runs this corner or that corner—is coming to an end." He puts his fists on the table in front of him and leans forward. "Between us in this room, we control every moving part of what's left in this city. We know each other. We may not like each other, but we know what each is about," He coughs twice and spits loudly into a bucket near his feet. "And what they can do.

"I don't know about you, but I'm tired of going hungry and drinking shit liquor." A few clap but everyone murmurs, remembering single malts, full bellies, happy children. "What started as a community of survivalists has morphed into a shootout that has left us with four. The Bordwells, Racks, Dozers, and the Fan Club." He looks us over.

"We know how we started. Sanitation engineers. Water purity specialists. Nurses, bakers, postal workers, everything in between. But," he sighs and coughs twice. "But a few years ago, we had to adapt. We developed new skills. Skills that have kept us alive, despite the poison in our air and the betrayal of our State. We became thugs, thieves, and liars. Most of us still are." A few people laugh and I join a handful who sport proud smiles, then shift my feet and quietly clear my throat. Burc waits for the murmur to die down, then just stands there, looking at us. He sniffs the air, stalks back and forth, moving from one set of eyes to the next.

"But *all* of that is going to change. Just a few hours ago, there was a hit on the Bordwells, and they reacted as they do." I wonder what they did. "If you and your people want to act like cowboys, only out for you and yours," a deep, wheezing breath. "You either check yourself right the fuck now, or be prepared for the rest of us to rain molten lead down your throats. The shit stops *now*." He breathes slowly, looking us over, trying to catch his breath.

"There's too much at stake here. Do you want to risk life and limb for antibiotics, sugar, flour, or a slab of butter?"

He pauses and I think about the Backseat Gunslinger's head evaporating. "We're running out of time. I can see and hear it in you, just as you can hear it in me," he wheezes, struggling to finish. "*I* need things, just as *you* do. I can't get those things, just as you can't. But we—*we*—" he raises his voice but a coughing fit cuts him off.

30 seconds pass and he's drooling into the bucket and spitting when he can. He's a dangerous shade of red when he's handed an inhaler. It clicks twice and dispenses life, but the third yields nothing. He throws it in the bucket. The red is fading to pink and his breathing seems to right itself.

"There's only one group not present here," he's standing straight, looking at each of us in turn. "One we all know, one we all hate. We've all clipped our fair share of them, but it's not been enough. Nothing we've done so far has been enough. We know this.

"We know how we started. They started the same way— but make no mistake, they are not like us. They started with the upper hand." He breathes twice. "But now, their grip is slipping. Tonight, our hand is stacked. Tonight, we start playing our cards." A rustle goes through the crowd that brings me back to New Hampshire. "We'll meet outside, squad up, and debrief in the cars."

More than a decade ago, a picnic with my grandparents and my older sister. We were walking down to a sycamore tree in the middle of a meadow, it was the middle of summer and we'd worked up a bit of a sweat walking and carrying the sandwiches, blankets, a bottle of burgundy and a carton of apple juice. I had paused and looked at the tree, and just then a breeze picked up and swam through the reedgrass, bringing it alive.

"Burc's a sycamore," I say to myself as everyone heads to the door. Their shoulders broader, chins held higher, their drunkenness, hunger and addictions hidden behind masks of pride and solidarity. Cam catches my gaze and her eyebrows jump once. I nod as we exit. I glance back and Riley's behind us in the hallway, eyes ahead and in his own world, chewing on his lip. There's a calmness to him I like.

"I gotta stop smokin," he muses as we step outside and lights one up. We're waiting for three cars to be loaded with the goods. Two people are running gallon jugs of gas from inside the building to two other people who are pouring them in with the care of a surgeon. Six others load plastic bags and boxes into trunks. Three men, fingers on triggers, stand on each side of the path from the school to the cars. Cam walks up to the closest three and asks a few quick questions.

Riley offers me a cigarette. I take it and motion for a lighter, run my thumb over the groove and bring the flame to my face. I inhale deeply, exhale, and as Cam walks back up to us, my mind unhinges and fingers tingle. I shake my head with a small smile and offer the cigarette to a giggling Cam. She shrugs and takes it.

"American Spirits?" She observes, exhaling slowly and handling the head rush of a non-smoker better than I ever could. She hands it back after another drag and the three of us share a smile.

"Hey," Riley starts, "I gotta get rid of something." He fishes around his pockets, "Do me a favor?" He asks, holding out a black-matte flask. I hand the cig back to Cam and take a sip, the smile on my face spreads through my body.

"And you're trying to get rid of this because . . .?" Cam trails off.

Riley squints as smoke floats into his eyes and in front of his face. "Tonight's—"

he stops, a smile creeping up the side of his mouth. "Tonight's gonna be solid. Crew seems tight, gear is top notch, haven't heard shit from the State in a few days—I mean, it's just—"

"Let's not start jinxing ourselves here," Cam jokes, sipping again.

"No such thing as luck, pretty lady." He takes a deep breath. "If you prepare enough—"

"If you prepare enough, you can what? You can dodge lightning?" I interrupt. He responds with an unimpressed look and half a laugh. "Catch the meteor and chuck it back? Avoid the earthquake? Avoid the—"

"Drone strike?" Cam tries to joke. Our smiles die and Riley takes the flask from her.

He takes a long sip and we stand for moment. "We used to be able to," he says, "but about eight months ago, the State changed to smaller drones with modified propellers to reduce sound." He shakes his head and I see his eyes take him some place else. "They even changed the cameras. We shot one down about, maybe, two months ago? They're using some new magnetic imaging lens we've never seen before, peeks right through everything except concrete and steel. That's why," he drops his cigarette, crushes it with a toe, pulls out another and lights it. "We've holed up here lately," pointing to the brick and mortar school.

The weight of reality surges through me, smashing the buzz of tobacco and plunging me into an ocean of whiskey and memory. I see both of them swimming in their own minds, drenched in blood, screams, and fear. We hold our silence for a few minutes as the final pieces around us fall into place. The air begins to hum.

I inhale and look at both of them in turn. I exhale and patiently unholster each Glock 20 beneath my arms. I rack the slide back on each of them, loading a round in each chamber. I untuck the .38 from my right sock, spin the cylinder then snap it back into place. "Let's just get this done."

We finish off the flask, each one swig in turn, as Burc comes out flanked by two men, one of them holding an AK and the other leaning on a nailed baseball bat with a .357 on his hip. He speaks slowly, with the same deliberate weight from before. "In the Civic: Riley, Cameron, Chestnut, Davey and Vick." He looks at each of them in turn. "In the Polo: Shelise, Anna, Kevin, Jules, Popeye. In the Focus: Terrance, Stephan, Irene, Eddie, Brandon." No one moves as he looks us over.

I see his thin frame and patchwork hair, and think of the sycamore. Its wide trunk and profuse crown look nothing like the old, sick man in front of me. "Alright," he says, and I'm in the shade of the leaves, the inescapable sun avoided for a time. He claps his hands once, turns around and walks inside.

I squeeze Cam's shoulder and she lands a few playful punches in my ribs. Riley gives me a two finger salute and disappears into the Civic just before her.

Hellos are nodded as we file in. The first thing I notice is that Eddie is fat and already sweating. He sits in the front with a sawed-off in his lap, four grenades on his lapel and a machete on his back. His beard is impressive and his smile huge, but he shows no teeth. "Everybody in?" Deep, husky, like an elephant. "Don't forget, click it or ticket!" We all smile and put our seatbelts on.

Brandon's driving. He's bald and the veins in his head stick out a bit too far. Irene sits in next to me, on my other side is Terrance. She's got an Uzi strapped to her chest and two phosphorus grenades linked to her ribs. I want to ask her where she got them when Terrance chimes in, his left knee jittering up and down: "Gonna be a fun one, ya?" He keeps looking at me for a response.

"You know it."

His eyes light up: "Heard the State's not shit now, not anymore, no. That's why Burcs, ah—" he licks his lips and rolls his head around, speaking fast and getting faster. "That's why he, he uh—you know, planned all this. Gonna finally get us a leg up on'em. Us. *Us!* So wild, to think of it? Think of it! *Us!* When has there been that! I mean—"

"Terry," Brandon tries, pulling the car out.

"I mean, just look at this crew alone—this car alone! You know—"

"Terry," he tries again, louder, the car speeding up.

"We know about you, you and Cam. We-we knew this was gonna be f-fu-*fun* when you guys and the Bordies were locked in. They even—"

"*Terry!*" he shouts.

Terry hits the chair in front of him. "A *minute*! A fuckin

104

minute!" He licks his lips again and his head twitches as he looks at me, peering through my whiskey. "Something big starting tonight here, Stephy," he finishes with a yellow smile.

"Stephan," I say, readjusting my legs and hips.

"Once he starts," Eddie offers as Terry rocks gently back and forth, rubbing his thighs with his palms. "He's hard to stop."

"He's the smallest, heaviest train you'll ever see," Irene says, looking out her window. Terry's holsters are on the front of his shoulders, strung across his chest. He has two automatic 9 millimeters with extended clips. There's a drum magazine sitting on his lap, its two large round chambers feeding into a small magazine linking them. I look at him as we accelerate and he's chewing his lips, gripping his knees.

"Alright," Brandon starts, turning his head but keeping his eyes ahead. "Two crews went ahead about three hours ago. They took the boats to set charges on the roadblocks at the end of the bridge. They're going to wait until we're close enough to blow the block. It'll be a bit dusty, but the bridge's more than big enough for all of us to play."

"Charges on the bridge?" Irene leans forward.

"Near the bridge," Brandon says without looking away from the road.

"Still, it's—"

"Pretty close," Terrance and Eddie say in unison, their voices colliding in bizarre harmony.

"Aren't the boats too loud for a run that close to the checkpoint?" I offer and am greeted with silent looks and eyebrows notched in contemplation.

"Ah ah ah, that's a, that's a good—you know, those old diesels never ran quiet before, now they're probably like a pack of dogs."

Eddie looks at each of us in then turns back into his seat. "Well," he cocks his shotgun. "Whatever."

"After the charges blow," Brandon continues, "we're gunning it until we reach the guardhouse. The cars will be single file. Eddie and Irene, sweep right. Me and Terry, sweep left. Stephan, you're over the top." I raise my eyebrows and push two laughs through my nose with a cleft smile.

"The top?"

He looks at me in the dirty rearview with a smile that makes me like him. "You got it. Cars'll be bumper to bumper, though. No hopscotch for you tonight."

"Now you're just killin the fun for me."

Brandon smiles, Irene gives me a nudge while Eddie and Terry share a laugh.

"What're we lookin at for time?" Irene asks through a smile.

"Five, six minutes. We're close," Brandon answers.

The rest of the ride is silent. I sink into my seat and flex every joint in my body, starting with my toes. I get past my hips and start rotating my shoulders backward when a trio of blasts bring everyone's hands to their guns.

"*Woop woop!* Here we go!" Brandon yells. We're maybe fifty yards from the growing cloud of brown and gray. Small pebbles start raining down on the car, one stars the windshield in front of Eddie. We speed into the cloud and Brandon whips the wheel left. "Seat belts!" We unlock and he's pumping the breaks and there's a pistol in my right hand. We're on the bridge and can see nothing, but I can hear Brandon's voice. We hit a bump and he counts to seven, then hits the brakes. Before we stop, doors open and feet are pounding ground.

I'm behind Irene, palm open and behind her back, smirking, foot up on a bumper, trunk, roof, hood. Trunk, roof, hood, and sprinting towards a bright room with everyone milling about.

By the time I'm in the room it's half empty and everyone else is on their way out the other side. Two people are rifling through papers, another trying to turn a computer on. I see Cam say something to Riley in the far corner near a row of dead monitors. As I walk up, he turns around not seeing me, holstering his weapon and shaking his head. My eyes are wide with fight and Cam's crooked with concentration. I holster my Glock, with a smile slap her on the arm: "Shit was—"

"Wrong," she whispers, shaking her head, "something's wrong."

"What?"

"I can—I smell cigarettes. The—"

"We just had one with—"

"It's different, it's in the air, it's really fresh—"

"Look, don't, we—"

"Feel the monitors." I sigh and look at the ceiling then place my hand on the glass then on the plastic casing. The warmth brings my eyes to hers, which were already shuffling around the mess left on the desk. "Five minutes, maybe ten, at the most," she whispers. "This is pretty weird—"

"What should we do?"

"Let's just get to the Dozers, we're pretty exposed if we just hang around here. Rally everyone up, I'll set up a perimeter outside while we get the cars through.

"Alright fellas!" I yell, "Easy enough! Let's head out! Dozers are waiting, let's finish the run and see what they got for us!" I slap the desk twice and I meet Cam's eyes before walking out. The cars are weaved through the zig-zag of concrete roadblocks of the checkpoint. Cam walks about, pointing and talking, her finger on the trigger.

We exchange useless words, talking like we won something, but the possibility of havoc and death rest in the air like static before lightning. All I can think about is the half apple I shared with Cam before we left Kevin, how it was soft, brown, and barely sweet.

As the cars weave through, the chatter dies down and we mill about, eyes down both streets, silently happy there wasn't a fight. Riley's huge smile reassures me about something, but Cam's unconvinced. We begin to slowly file back in our cars and head down empty roads. The bridge is only fives minutes to Church Street.

"Ed—Ed—hey Ed?"

"Hm?"

"Wanna kick it there for a bit? Those, those—"

"Girls'll sure be happy to see us."

"You boys," Irene chides with a fake motherly tone.

"Don't act like they don't have your poison too, missy," Brandon teases, sniffing the air twice.

"What about you, St-Stephy?" I get a few elbows.

I look to my left and say with a slow smile, "Liquor."

"All that and so much more when we get to church," Eddie laughs and his body rocks the car. "Best place in the universe, save Miletus."

"Hah! Never thought you'd believe in the shit the State spews out." Brandon chides.

Eddie looks at him, sounding confident but not pushing the issue. "Dunno, man. Heard some stories about Apeiron and the whole thing sounds pretty legit. Bordwells like to pump out their own fictions, but lotta stories been matchin up from people who never known each other."

Cam and I exchange a glance. Everyone knows the rumors of the way out, but it all sounded just as absurd as the propaganda the Bordwells pushed.

"The thirstiest of men will find sanctuary in even the most absurd mirages," Brandon ends the conversation with a friendly slap on Eddie's chest and walks to his car. The silence around us thin with hope, but the reality of scummy streets, sewage tinted air and not a single plant in sight is too heavy to carry the conversation further.

The streets in Harvard Square are narrow. Most lights are out, fires abandoned as the convoy passes. Everything is a husk. What's left alive has a large red ball painted on it. It's meant be a wrecking ball, but it looks like an old cartoon bomb.

A block before we turn right onto Church Street, the gutters change and abandoned cars disappear. We make a slow turn right and a roadblock halfway through the street stops us. There are people in an adjacent parking lot, a few tents popped with lights going.

"Well lookey here," Irene thinks out loud, leaning forward for a better look.

"Everybody seems nice and friendly," Eddie observes. Brandon sits and watches a group of five men go through the security motions with the two cars ahead.

"They do when they have their v-vice."

Our turn's up and we get out. Four guards are all wearing the same gear: M4 rifle, flak jacket, machete, and a Glock 20 similar to mine. Theirs look newer. The fifth carries a revolver on his hip, an MP7 on his back, a clipboard in his hands. A large duffle bag rests at his feet. Brandon removes each weapon and each magazine. The magazine and rounds go in one bag, the weapon itself in another. He asks Brandon his name, scribbles, looks at the numbers on the bags, scribbles again.

Cam's waiting past the roadblock already. She smiles, puts her index and middle finger on either side of her mouth and flicks her tongue a few times before turning and walking toward the church. I laugh and two of the guards stare at me.

Irene's finished, following Brandon to the final frisk. Terry's jittery and having trouble unlatching the drum magazine. Eddie steps once to help and gets a barrel pointed at his chest. I don't move and wait out the fight between unstable fingers and disagreeable latches. The magazine's finally free and his scream of relief makes us laugh and the guards smile.

I disarm last, slowly removing the extra clips on my hips and lower back. The clipboard is scribbled on, I'm nodded forward. The frisk is quick, and from a familiar face.

"Hey," said with a real smile. "Been a while." It's Byron.

I return the greeting. "No more running with us, eh?"

He shakes his head. "Can't keep up with you guys anymore. This is," he looks around, "not the fast life by any means, but," he shrugs. "Heard it's better than firefighting out west." He still has the two polished bronze bracelets his wife made him. He sees me notice them and puts his hands in his pockets. "It's a—I'm shot at a whole lot less." He laughs and won't look me in the eyes. I wonder how he actually got in with the Dozers. "Cam's still looking good," he offers.

"Always does, man. Well—"

"Oh! I got someone for you to meet."

"Yeah?"

"Yeah—Sasha. She's inside, ask Mark."

"Mark?"

"Yup. Big black dude, scar on the arm."

"He's the one who fought—oh, fuck, who was it? He fought—"

"Donny?"

"Donny! Yeah!" Almost three years ago. "Yeah, and he was reciting—"

"—poems the whole damn time!" We share a laugh that's swallowed by the night. "Alright man," he starts again.

"Yeah. I'll catch ya inside? Bump a line or two?"

Byron steps aside so I can pass and he slaps me on the back. "Maybe. I'm here for a bit. Gonna be a busy night."

"Oh? Who else you got rolling through?"

"Ah, you know," he coughs. "Same old folk, can never get enough of what they don't need."

I start walking backwards, looking at him. "If you get some time,"

"Whiskey—"

"—neat—"

"And coke."

We smile one last time and wave. I turn, walk. My lack of pistols puts a kick in my step and I feel light and alive.

I reach the side door of the church where two women stand and I can sense the life they're guarding behind them.

"Burc's crew?" One asks, hand already on the door.

"Yeah," I thumb over my shoulder and turn to look at the cars. They're collapsing part of the roadblock and driving them over into the parking lot. People are starting to clump up, ready to unload the trunks.

I turn back and they're holding the large double door open. I step through and the smells hit me as I turn left and follow the stairs down. Incense, sweat, tobacco. Halfway down and the sounds begin. Stories, laughter, bodies moving. At the bottom of the stairs I walk through a curtain to my

J. Gray

right and see what it means to be alive.

Half the crew is here, mixed with ten or so other people I don't know, the rest and more probably split between the five or six rooms that line the walls.

Cam's making out with a girl—black tank top riding up, half-shaved head, tattoos of something lining her neck and right arm. A thin man is crafting and recrafting lines of white powder on a table in front of them. Brandon's smoking and talking to a group of people.

At the center of the room is a round table. In the middle are bottles—whiskey, wine, vodka, even tequila. Along the edges are decorated wooden boxes. I open one and there's a bunch of sealed plastic bags, all with the same small collection: alcohol swab, two brown tabs, a syringe, five matches. I put the box down where I found it, next to two smaller boxes filled with spoons and foot long elastics. I survey the bottles, grab a cup and a half full bottle of Jameson.

I pour, sit, and sip. Cam looks at me as she bites on the girl's lip. I raise my glass with a smile. She stops the girl from going into her pants with a sad smile, then leans to the thin man, who lifts a mirror with a straw.

I lean back and think about lost flour, melted butter, and how this can't last much longer. Cam slumps next to me, eyes wide and alive.

"Who here," she says, taking the bottle from between my legs and taking a sip. "Has the biggest cock?".

"Twitchey McGee," I nod at Terrance, who's tying off his arm in a far corner, laying on a bed of pillows with three other people.

"You have an eye for these things," she laughs and sips again.

"You look like you're feeling better. You looked crampy as hell back before we left."

"Yeah," she stands, "only so much fun for me tonight," walks and examines the table.

I tilt my head back and let the sounds of life carry me away on my ferry of whiskey. Someone sits next to me and I put my around them.

"Hey," a voice like small boots on gravel that isn't Cam's. I look and a pair of hazel eyes framed by curly black hair rest above a soft, round nose and parted lips.

"You're Steven?"

"Close enough," I answer.

"What?" She leans back and her smile transforms her face from beautiful to unforgettable.

"It's Stephan, but—"

"Well," she tries to hide the smile and looks away, playing with an ebony curl, her profile chiseling itself in my memory. "I'm glad you finally made it here." I waited for her to continue. "Your crew spends so much time on the other side of the river, we only get to see the same faces." She leans forward and licks her lips.

"Well, I—"

"Will take a break from your everyday heroics and make a few memories with me?" Her arm is on my shoulder and hand on the bottle which she grabs and takes a swig from, leaning back and closing her eyes. She tops my cup off then walks to the opposite side of the table, searching. She looks back to see me staring. She turns around, eyes down, and leans forward, pushing her elbows together. I sip and watch her walk back.

My arm is around her waist and we walk to a room and I'm on my back with my shirt off and her tongue dancing with mine. Her shirt's off and my hands are on her tits, her hips rocking and getting me hard. She slows, leans down and kisses me once, crawling backward.

My elbows prop me up and she's at the end of the bed, smiling, curls long and messy. Her tongue flicks out and there's something small and white on it, it's bitter as she presses it into my mouth. Her thighs against my hips, she leans for the bottle, holds it to her lips but doesn't swallow. She brings her full mouth to mine and releases a wave of whiskey down my throat, cheeks and chin.

My wrists are in her hands and above my head, she's

catching what whiskey she can with her lips, she moves to my chest, her mouth cold and amazing. My heart jumps as my pants are undone and she kisses my stomach. I'm in her mouth, the cold of her lips erased by the warmth of her throat and I don't know where I am. Her curls, soft and clean, head moving up and down, the build up shortening my breath. I lurch slightly, breathing quicker, starting to sweat. I groan, inhale, but can't. I can't breathe.

I force all the air from my lungs and try to suck in again. My head is pounding and my dick is about to explode down her throat. After a third attempt and failure to breathe I push her away from me and the pressure is building behind my eyes. I sit forward—my pills—my jacket—I'm looking at the ceiling, her hands on my chest, I push, sit forward again and something rocks my head to the right.

Everything is black and gray and there is an inferno in my lungs. Something's dripping, running down my face and neck. I hear only my erratic heartbeat.

Infantile breaths seep into me. I fall from the bed. I drag myself to the door, collapse, looking right. My jacket is light years away. The walls are breathing and the dingy, stiff carpet is the most sensuous thing I've ever felt. I collapse from my elbows, my cheekbones relishing the fabric and eyes greeting what's left of Eddie's head. It's gone from the nose up and his beard is matted with blood and pink chunks, but it's okay. I'm okay. I breathe deeply and melt into the floor.

The skinny man next to Cam has a smashed mirror for a face and is sweating blood. The girl Cam was kissing is now hugging her neck with both arms. Cam's face is the color of the cop after she found the yeast and *I didn't want to kill her, I didn't want to kill her, I didn't want*—someone walks in front of Cam with shiny wrists and brings fists to her face again and again and my stomach sinks through the floor and I see a flurry of black curls walk through the door, it lifts a knee and there's a massive foot that smashes my face, rises, smashes my face, rises, smashes my face until everything is gray and the carpet is ignorant of my embrace.

The Beast

This is a place where whores and junkies come to die.

Just as a dog will separate itself from the pack and a cow from the herd, so too do nightcrawlers of the most foul type.

A thin security guard who stalks me into the building, where I see an empty room with the door open and the light on, stares at me with his hands hovering about his waist. There's a TV on in the hallway blaring about a bombing in Times Square, probably watched by the 50-something clerk who got the very wrong idea when I asked her what's her favorite fish from the market two blocks down. The guard waits for me to pass then steps into the hall to see what room I'm in. Ants, flies, open windows to let in the chaotic orchestra of dog fights, an unflushable toilet with my piss still in it, unable to escape. A mirror placed perfectly at the far end of the bed. Pussy pink walls. A thin film over everything that makes me feel like everything decent is dead or dying. Hourly rates for rooms—no one wants to stay here longer than they need to. I jerk off twice and rinse my dick in the sink. There's no drain for the shower. Only a bucket. The pillows feel like fresh horse intestines. It just stopped raining.

The upside down, empty but not clean ashtray is the only attempt at cleanliness. The soap is wrapped in a sheet of single ply toilet paper and there's no roll in the bathroom. I'm pretty sure fleas have been biting me and I start to scratch but stop instantly when a cat yelps, telling the world it's ready to be fucked.

I sweat, but this isn't normal sweat. It's sludge. Coaxed out from clogged pores by the 4 walls around me, holding on to the scent of desperation and sex that will never be aired from the room. The only things I can think of are crumpled, damp dollar bills and the fleeting eyes that don't want to meet after doing something embarrassing and necessary. There's purple trim on the floors and ceilings. I drink warm water and my arms stick to the table as I write.

The mirror is large and plays tricks on me. A slight breeze or page flip catches my breath and I think I see it again. The gelatinous beast I saw lug its way onto the beach as the tides rolled in. There are voices outside and it sounds like English, but why risk speaking to them, telling them what I saw. They won't believe me. I write to push it from my mind, but here, now, it has still taken hold. The mass of moving tentacles and folds had an intelligence and an unstoppable appetite to it, too. It was moving with the tides, lurching forward and ebbing back, finally breaching land when a chance lightning bolt caught everyone's eyes. I stalked it then, as it does me now, as it will crawl around your spine and shoulders soon enough.

It went for the weak and the small first, those animals that evolved ignorant of the caress and remain unaware of its absence even now. The stray cats no one cares about, the dogs who beg most attentively and fight each other like it will give them a home. The mantis and the crane, the monkey and the ant, and everything in between. These it catches and devours easily, a whip from a single tentacle and their simple minds are simpler still, but no longer their own.

Next it consumes those humans that are not children and not yet adults, for their minds are also simple and their bodies willing. The beast takes some time with these, but not much, and is still amazingly adept. I sit hunched, eyes wide and fists tight as I see the beast force them into their awkward, wanting, yet unknowing dances. An odd rhythm is pervasive and it's obvious the steps of something more gentle is beyond their comprehension. The fault is with their parents, or their history, or both, but it's obvious our youngest have a terrifying lack of patient sensuality. They start to pirouette and the beast slithers on. I follow and watch.

Those not yet defeated by age, with sense and faculty, the most dexterous version of our flawed species, prime themselves for each other. Seeing the beast mangle the minds and torture these bodies fills me with a horrible, enticing awe and I'm unable to look away. The numberless tentacles weave between and through individuals and groups with ease, and I'm excitedly stunned no one seems to realize, though I notice how everyone feels it. With slime-ridden limbs everywhere, the beast executes its complicated waltz as partners are found, lost, and found again. It's here I sense, at some incredibly primal level, in the marrow of my bones and the very base of my spine, what this thing is doing. I see the animal that the beast is grinding to extinction, I hear the snapping of its bones and popping of its joints and smell the breath of its death rattle. I also sense the delight of the beast and follow it, watching.

It seems reluctant with the final choreography, it's noticeable with the languid movements. But the primal fire in it still burns, I can tell, by the deftness of its motions, subtle and deliberate. This, it seems, is the line dance of familiarity for those contemplating what will be writ on their tombstones. The beast moves slowly because it is certain of its success over the now ancient animal that would purr and play with these, the final dancers.

As the line dance closes, my fists are tighter still and I feel the gaze of the beast upon me. I will not succumb. I have seen what this thing does to others and I cannot fall victim as well. I sprint from the shore, my lungs and body burning, and I can feel, almost, that I've lost it. Two blocks before reaching the room described above, and I slow, to not arouse suspicion from the guard or the attendant.

But as I slow I feel its presence, its slither, its undeniable mass not close and not far behind me. I shut the door and begin writing, and now you are present with me, for my undeniable fall, one that you will eventually surrender to as well, but hopefully long after the words here are finished. I can hear it now, slapping at my door, my mind growing weak. I fight but I know the futility. I look out my window at all those dancing, and surrender, letting it die in me as I begin my third.

The Shapeless Storm

The downpour is upon the strangers
through the streets they sprint
testing every door until one gives.
A bar—only spirits with an old man
whose shaky wrists grip a shotgun.

They wipe their faces and shake their hands.
An errant drop,
glistening with sapphire, ruby and emerald
flies high on to the window
that separates them from the torrents
washing everything away.

All three stand and stare
at the peculiar drop
and its backdrop of chaos.

It begins to slide, slow at first
leaving a trail in which the strangers see
reflections of silence and escape.

The barman bites down
thunder masks the report and his tumble.
Lightning shatters the window
the strangers fall together with glass in their eyes
as the pale blue dot
rejoins the shapeless storm.

Clarity

Through the fog of our fathers
we see only hills, vaguely.

We walk trails cut by them
while burning their maps,
smashing statues

devouring their libraries and
dismantling ceremonies
to embers and ash.

The fog matures to rain.
The hills are mountains of pitch
preserving vibrant green.

we were all so important. every letter J. Gray
of our cosmically abnormal story mattered,
like every voice was on the cusp of harmonizing

Corporal Carlyle

when we began our tumble.

Six days after his son's death and three after the funeral, Jonas Carlyle is almost finished buying everything he
needs for the last thing he will ever do. He sits in front of a
library computer after writing down the necessary numbers,
too scared to go home and fill the silence with only himself.
He finishes the adjustments to the new cordless telephone
as he finishes the orders and agrees on pickup dates. Two
days pass as Jonas drives to Philadelphia for a pickup, then to
Lodi, a town about an hour away from Trenton, for another.
Two more pass as he mixes the components in his garage and
sets them in place.

Jonas' phone is blissfully ignored in his front right
pocket as he walks the aisles of a hardware store. Its vibrating
is incessant. Fingering the piece of paper in his left pocket,
he pauses in front of the cashier, looking at the hammer and
chisel. After bringing up a single extended index finger and
making eye contact with her, he walks away and comes back
with another chisel. He takes his change and walks out.

Finally confronting the house—but not acknowledging
the silence—Jonas walks with speed and intent, gathering
what he needs through the depressingly familiar arrangement of furniture. The smell of home slows his feet but the
silence pushes him on. He keeps his eyes away from pictures
of picnics, vacations, dinners and cookouts. He doesn't dare
touch the plastic flamingos from their honeymoon, dangling
in a kitchen window with the sun slowly eating their pink to
white. The wind chime sings from the back porch and Jonas'
stoicism fails him. He walks into their room and he doesn't
wipe the tears from his face.

the cataclysm began in the streets.

Only the oldest and dingiest clothes suffice. His old Army jacket, stripped of its CARLYLE tag. Originally tan, now brown work boots. Tattered painters pants. An old green and white Christmas sweater. He removes his father's watch but not his ring. He doesn't remember the last time he showered or shaved. Stashing the chisels in the side pockets of his jacket and tucking the hammer between his pants and lower back, Jonas walks out of his bedroom only to come back in a few seconds later, grabbing his guitar case.

Jonas slides his guitar into the backseat and flops behind the wheel. Arms, body and face momentarily statuesque in absolute grief and determination. Before starting the engine, he takes the folded paper from his pocket and puts it to the left of the speedometer so he can see it as he drives, the childish letters visible but indiscernible. Turning the key, he realizes he doesn't want it that far away and puts it in the breast pocket of his jacket, where it sits heavier than the hammer and chisels.

The drive in is slow with waves of traffic. A motorcycle in the breakdown lane blows past him and its backfire makes Jonas jump and tense every muscle in his body. He breathes quickly for a minute then counts to twenty, slowing with each breath. Both hands grip the bottom of the wheel, waiting for those ahead to move. Jonas' mind refuses to be kind. It forces him to remember tender moments of care and anger and pride and when the line of mechanical coughers driven by mechanical thinkers finally moves, his face is wet and his hands are fists on the wheel.

He isn't sure of how long he'd been driving, but Jonas realizes he's in the city. He parks the car five blocks east of the destination in an alleyway along Lexington Avenue where it'll stay until stolen or the buildings around it crumble. The brick face of a building is chipped where Jonas slams the door open and maneuvers out. The bubbling in his stomach tells him he needs something in it if he wants to keep going. He is always hungry but can never eat.

A cafe comes up on his left, Oren's Daily Roast, and

he enters, asking for a cup of hot water—no he doesn't need a lid, no he doesn't need the protective sleeve, no he doesn't care about the bewildered look of employees or the shuffling steps customers take to put subtle distance between them and him. He starts toward the door then stops and puts the cup to his lips.

Top lips curl up in fearful disdain as the eyes that observe an unkempt, unshaven, unwashed *something* pour scalding water down its throat. He doesn't drink it, just lets it fall. Pain is simply there, easily ignored, resting on the surface like a latex glove.

Out the door, three blocks to go, guitar strap beginning to dig in his shoulder and remind him it's there. Hollow grief burns in his chest, mocking the heat from the water. Jonas' pace slackens for a moment as he realizes the heat and the pain are the first things he's felt since watching his son be buried. He wants another cup, but his legs won't stop, the machine of his body operating its own gears and joints.

The rusty iron of memories slow him. The placid faces at the funeral embed themselves in the scaffolding of his bones. He sees their waxen faces in the lowered gazes of people walking past him and they render the hollow grief into feverish machinations.

The city around him is gone and Jonas sees only the foundational crack that ran through his wife's face as she stood opposite of him. They caught each other's eyes as a supposed man of God spoke cliche words of returning and ascending and amending and that look between them set in place like gears flowing into each other. Over their dead son's body they had their last moment together. The gears kept turning and both of them offered their sacrifices of water to the soil in which their seed was resting. Looking down at what was left of their own rearranged flesh and blood, boxed and ready to be buried, they were pulled apart from each other by the undeniable progress of time.

Rising from his reverie, Jonas realizes he's stopped at the corner and is staring at the stone. Jonas knows he wouldn't—

couldn't—let anyone forget this moment, this grief, this child. His child.

Staring.

This is it.

He sits and opens his guitar case and begins hitting any chords that feel familiar. West 42nd street and 7th Avenue meet at a corner, Times Square, and here Jonas sits, rolling lifeless fingers over vibrating strings as herds of people move about, each with some semblance of a destination. They walk with long strides and open but unreceptive eyes. Jonas stops making noise and decides to get to work.

He squeezes the tools and the city with its sea of people disappears again. He is back in the delivery room: he has his wife's hand in both of his and they are screaming in tandem, excited to near hysteria, exuberant in blinding pain and celebrating the first seconds of their complete union. With the first infantile wails, Jonas' second half stops screaming and her spasms cease as she transcribes that energy into her newborn son, who takes the helm of noise-making. Jonas falls into a stupor of selflessness that he didn't know existed before this moment, a complete abandonment of his self possible only through dedication fueled by love. He tries to squeeze her hand and look at the first time mother, but instead Jonas is squeezing his tools and staring into a listless mass of moving bodies.

With his back to the dead stone and the living sea in front of him, Jonas strikes the first vertical line, a diagonal one half the length of the first, then a connecting mirror image of the first two lines. It is an eternal tattoo that everyone will read, that everyone will remember. The spine of following letters are hammered out by the clay-faced artisan, the defeated father, the ignoring and the ignored operating amidst each other, the former fighting through transient faces and the latter unable to forget one.

Maxima is completed, and Jonas rewards himself with vibrations from his guitar. His fingers fall over the strings and his mind ventures inward through the labyrinth of memory, doors seared shut with tears and hallways decorated with easy smiles and lazy Sunday afternoons.

It was spring, almost-summer, when the warm days tease you with cool breezes on your forearms and sunny hugs from behind, when temperatures shift and mix, changing like tea steeping in a pot, leaving no one smileless. The three of them were in the backyard, Cynthia had made a lengthy, affectionate goodbye to run inside and check her email and would only be gone a few minutes. The sound of the door sliding shut was met with the boy asking, in his beautiful youth, what was in the brown bottle Jonas was holding, christened with the slightest glaze of condensation. Jonas let him hold the bottle and smiled at the surprise that walked across his soft cheeks at the weight, and the grimace that marched through his eyes after he brought the bottle from his lips and handed it back, shaking his head fiercely. Cynthia walked back out, smiling, her hands anxious to get back around Jonas, who stifled a laugh when he heard his boy burp.

Debetur is done. Jonas can't remember when his hands stopped playing and started carving again, but things like these aren't questioned anymore. Things just happen. Sometimes you know why, other times you can only raise your and eyes to the sky and ponder at the infinity. *P*, *u*, and *e* were just finished when one of the anonymous few who've unplugged from the game of money and cosmetic happiness steps out of the sea and notices Jonas.

"This isn't your fuckin corner," he says. "So get the fuck out." The skin on his face is sunburnt and plagued with a perpetual look of slight confusion and derision. His eyes aren't afraid to look and his mouth delights in describing what most don't want to hear. It is his corner. Jonas pauses and lets the hammer and chisel fall to the ground. The Owner's head tilts to the side and he asks "Whaddaya got there?" A pause. The Owner of the corner knows Jonas won't respond, his mouth is as silent as his eyes. The Owner sees the empty guitar case and accepts the affront of Jonas taking his panhandling spot in stride, seizing an opportunity.

He clears his throat. "I've got a," he thinks. "A business proposition." He kneels down. "Nobody's gonna pay much attention if you just sit and strum them strings. You need someone," he chews his lower lip. "You need someone to be a front-man, somebody who can get that attention you know you want, and get that case filled up a bit." Jonas pauses for a second and looks at the man and is about to shake his head when he notices their jackets are the same.

The Owner's tag is still there: JONES. The green is more faded and the pockets torn. He's still wearing the standard issue boots, but the laces are gone. His eyes are brown but lighter than his skin and they stare into past blood and brotherhood as he looks at nothing in particular as he speaks. Jonas picks up the chisel and hammer and finishes the *r* and the *o* of *puero*.

"It's easy, man. We split everything. Fifty-fifty. Deal? Deal." The Owner clears his throat and puts his back to the stone, facing the same way as Jonas, looking out over the waves.

"Ladies!" he says, grabbing the attention of two women walking in opposite directions, wearing fisheye sunglasses and knee-high leather boots, who both look but keep walking. He passes his hand over the faded cypress tree on his shirt before beginning again. "Gentle—*men*—! If there are any left out there in this harsh, winding, windy, and wasteful world of ours!" His voice changes, his affect broad and clear, intonation inviting and annunciation crisp. The voice of a performer, or commander. People are looking as they pass, but none stop. "For a few paltry cents of your six and seven figure lives you can come and witness something great, something wonderful, something full of magic and honesty!" Two boys wearing backpacks stop, one Hispanic, the other Asian, and are the first.

"Ladies! Gentlemen! You are about to witness, if you so please, an invocation of the artist! I, one Montgomery Melpo Jones, will sacrifice my corporeal being to the whims of any of the nine sisters who've brought you all the strokes of genius

126

and masterful turns of phrase!"

"Don't taint those boy's minds—or those myths—with some fucking acid trip of yours, Monty." A beat cop, obviously familiar with the Owner of the corner, interrupts the scene and steps in front of the boys. Jonas shifts to his left, behind the Owner, sliding with chisel and hammer still in his hands which had begun to sweat. He puts the tools on the ground, sitting on them. A bolt of anger rips through his chest and he stares at his unknown brother, talking like a preacher and threatening his work. The Owner's shoulders slouch back to their accustomed posture of defeat.

"Go solve some real fuckin crimes, donut diva. I need to eat, and if the kids wanna hear a story, let'em listen. Besides, I'm about the Word now," he says as he pulls a cross of cypress hanging from his dingy neck on a shoelace as proof. "Devil outta me now," his voice lower, rubbing the crook of his right elbow.

"You watch your mouth," the cop says, taking a step forward and lowering his voice.

"Look, Samson," says the Owner, lowering his voice so the boys couldn't hear him. "This isn't some crazy shit I'm talking here. Learn up, shit's Greek, man! Look I'm trying, Samson, I'm trying! You know this ain't—"

"Right, right, right, Monty, I know, I know. Like I haven't heard this shit from you or anyone of you junky fuck ups," he looks at Jonas. The officer leans in, saying "keep the fuck away from those boys," in a whisper that's meant to be heard before turning and walking away.

Jonas looks up to see the cop walking away and the two boys waiting at a distance. He was through *r-e-v-e* before the interruption and begins again on the second *r*, his palms drying along with the threat of losing everything.

The Owner starts back up again, shoulders straight and proud, chin raised to accommodate the voice. "Ahem!" The Owner clears his throat with dramatic flair and it's a magnet to the boys. Jonas doesn't feel his hands stop or the anger in his belly evaporate into a mist of complete focus on every syllable and sound that flower from the stranger's mouth. He can feel his son near, and his attention is forced upon the stranger to the right, placating his grief. The Owner's voice rings out through the sea:

"Sit and search.
The sand that sifts through fists once
stood as the peak of a mountain top
worn and broken by wind
from Grandfather Clock's Hands
and their refusal to stop spinning.

Sit and ask:
who can navigate the gears?
Who tightens
the loosening bolt?

Sit and think:
Would you keep that mountain top for yourself?
Or would your hands hold you
humbled as hostage in the face
of laws that weren't written
of laws that simply are?

Sit and search.
Grab the bolt or grab the hammer?
Tighten and save or swing and defy
all that came before
and every strand
that might have been.

You cannot be the eternal rebel.
We walk under the mercy of those hands.
Mettle you may, for now.
Wander in wonder and may you be merry,
but you will never escape the need to
stand and decide."

Despite constant movement of the body and feet of the sea, silence manages to settle on the two boys and the Owner. The rhythm of Jonas' chisel starting up again melts into the white noise of detail. He has finished the spine of all 28 letters and is retracing them with his fingers, finding nicks to smooth and honing exact lines, maneuvering both hands behind his back. The Owner's shoulders liquefy back down to their normal, relaxed position and he tries to hustle a few dollars out of the boys. They're still transfixed in the moment, trying to understand what just happened and digest the system of words just spoken to them. The Hispanic boy reaches in his jeans pocket, the Owner already ignoring him—moving on to good old fashioned begging—not noticing both sets of young eyes still staring at his face. The boy drops in a soft piece of gum and a thick eraser, leaving his three quarters and a nickel in his other pocket. Both boys look at each other, bewildered, and walk away.

Jonas stops twice over the next five hours, swapping in the unused chisel for the finer details of the letters. Jonas barely notices the presence of this other, doesn't register the money in the case or the cut that's taken from his unsought-after partner. He doesn't feel himself sleep but assumes that he must. Whenever he swallows and there's a twang that he remembers is pain, he motions to the Owner for a cup of hot water, which is placed at his side a few minutes after his request. Half the reason for the water drinking is to keep the blood flowing in his hands, the warmth triggering something in his blood vessels, reminding his body that it's still working—somehow, somehow—and the other reason is to let the contents fall down his throat and into his stomach so it can sit and burn. A few passers-by think this is part of his act, that it worked somehow into his guitar playing. They attribute his boiled, wretched stare to his acting ability, ignoring the shiver of fear that drips down their spines as they walk.

Maxima debetur puero reverentia is finished and Jonas is tired of doing everything behind his back—of hiding his work, concealing his art.

He stands in the morning air, unaware of how long he'd been sitting, and arches his back, looking around. He is unseen. So is everything he's done. There is no reason to hide his tools and his work. His grey eyes pause on an all-blue sky. His clogged memory drags up images of a time when fighting for these people would bring him pride and happiness.

His hands trace over the completed words. The father levels his eyes and sees Freddy's face in the stone before making his first strike: noting the depth of the jaw, each line of hair, thin lips that curve on the right in a perpetual smirk, Cynthia's nose. The lucidity of the face that Jonas sees in the lifeless stone stirs a moment that sits unblemished in his mind forever.

The three of them, late summer, when the nights are cool but the ground is still hot from the day, and the early morning leaves traces of breath in front of your face, no . . . at first it was the two of them—him and Cynthia—a Monday morning, he was on leave and she had called out of work with plans of making love. They did. Cynthia hugging her knees with her head turned to the side, cheek resting on knee cap, looking at Jonas who was popper on an elbow. The love was slow and warm, the soul affirming sex that leaves you in a daze. Their gaze almost broke but the sound of Freddy waking up and talking to his action figures about what they were going to do for the day wouldn't let them look at anything but each other, until their young king ran into the room. Jonas wasn't aware moments like this could exist, the perfect harmonic string of events with each silver thread wrapping around the other, just like those three sets of arms around those three separate but forever together bodies.

A horn brays and the Owner of the corner tells Jonas that it's just a request for him to pick up his guitar. The only thing Jonas thinks about when he makes the first strike—almost diagonal, down from right to left—is how Freddy separated into a thousand pieces like a glass full of wine crashing to the ground. And how it was he who'd called him across the street.

Three days go by. The Owner gives a nudge whenever a cop comes within a block or so, and Jonas sits slowly, puts down his hammer and chisel to pick up his guitar. The cups of hot water become more frequent as general shapes begin to emerge from Jonas' slow work into the stone. The water becomes tea when the Owner finally notices the fine detail of a cheek, the wisps of hair and the globe of an eye.

Two more pass. Jonas tells the Owner he should leave, should walk away and keep going, and the odd display of emotion from the brick-faced man is made serious by the lifeless eyes and flat tone. It's almost an order. Jonas bends over and picks up the guitar to give it to him, and nudges the case with his foot. Montgomery nods and almost salutes when their eyes meet.

Every line is smooth, every pore and fold of skin rendered perfectly. In Jonas' pocket is the cordless home telephone, modified after the chemical purchases, ready to be used. He runs his left hand over his son's face and puts his right hand over his top left breast pocket. He stands and walks across the street to gaze at his son through the sea of anonymous bodies.

When Jonas presses the TALK button, five separate explosions will detonate the intersection around his son. The explosives are loaded in large Rubbermaid bins; three are packed in a specific manner with a high density plastic that will deflect the explosion, pushing the force of memory and anguish and guilt in very specific, calculated directions. When Jonas presses the TALK button, two buildings will be completely razed and three partially destroyed. 1,732 people will die and 439 will be injured, 22 permanently crippled. 1,587 airports will be shut down. Business around the country will cease for a full 14 hours. The whole world will pause for a moment to watch and ponder. When Jonas presses the TALK button, buildings will collapse in such a manner that standing in the center of a small crater will be the corner of a building with a young boy's face etched into it, with the words *maxima debetur puero reverentia* resting below the serene countenance. When Jonas presses the TALK button, he will walk into a wall of flame bearing only his love for a lost child and the knowledge that the world will forever know he existed.

Skull

How much does it weigh?
The idea left by the dock
that lived and died as a struck match.

There is a daunting forgetfulness
that drugs us all.

What we forget makes us
grow and burn and atrophy.

That chemical dance of orchestrated hurricanes
carries such cranial weight and sobriety
it buckles knees and send worms rushing.

we all share the same finish line
and because of this
we became

A Drop of Water

A man sits on the ground with his shoulders hunched, wrists trembling and hair gyrating in the wind like charred corn husks on a torched farm. His skin and clothes have been weathered to the same color and texture by innumerable days under the sun and rain, moon and snow. A faded patch on his jacket reads: JONES. His feet are shoeless and look like expensive leather. He watches weeds push their green frontier through the bricks in the sidewalk and wishes calamity upon the street poles whose bases are tickled by the nondescript life, he waits for the painted steel to teeter and collapse while the agonizing minutes of solitude build into towers of days and weeks. He wakes only to be ignored and thirsty.

The man's back is against a line in the contoured fingerprint of the metropolis, a granite wall a meter high that stretches for most of a city block. Imbedded in this wall are thousands of tall black metal spears welded together at the top and bottom, and upon every twelfth there perches a naked child angel with dwarven wings and lifeless stone eyes. Behind this barricade grows a wall of bushes trimmed daily and chosen specifically for the long curved barbs that decorate their stems. A dozen meters of lush manicured grass is growing behind these bushes and is populated with towns of birdbaths carved in the image of Greek gods, tiered bird feeders shaped like Buddha overflowing with organic seed imported from Madagascar and fountains shaped like lotus flowers that ejaculate and consume the same water in an intricate ballet the man will be forever ignorant of.

White walls that are cleaned by anonymous hands every two days stretch above and behind the fountains like crafted

what monsters and demons dream of

135

mountains overlooking shoddy anthills. From the windows a yellow hue bleeds into the night, stretching shadows of the lawn ornaments into a bizarre carnival of the ancient and the industrial, the modern and the natural while illuminating nothing but a fraction of the gulf between its pampered sources and the thirsty degenerate.

The light is delicate and fractured through the thousands of barely swaying crystals of three chandeliers and has a weak music all its own, echoes of which can be heard by passersby who steal glances through the erected barriers of space and life, a melody that reeks of traditions of blood and steel.

The carnival of shadows begins in earnest as the first dishes are served and three sets of mahogany doors painted burgundy with a deep forest green trim are shut and locked.

Inside, the floor is a glut of geometric intricacies. Three massive circular centerpieces are framed by an additional six—three on the left and right—whose varied fractal shapes act as borders then extend past, forging blossoms of complementary shapes, each line spawning hundreds of symmetrical bodies and gradual curves whose ratios are generic individually but elegant collectively. The ceiling is high and domed, the pillars leading to the center are ordained with vines and flowers whose immense craftsmanship goes ignored, as are the three murals that form the ceiling, all staring down at the patient gluttons.

One is a majestic yet erroneous amalgamation of many Greek and Roman gods, beginning on one side with a thin layer of blackness, the chaos from which all sprung, and ending with the beautiful Hermaphroditus pointing to the following piece. The mural is dominated by the tongueless Philomela, positioned in the center, crafting a tapestry upon which war and blood reign. An incredible dragon, Yinglong, or perhaps Longwei, faces the pointing figure as a shower of rain falls on its head and its gaping jaws are about to devour the young god or maybe its own tail, which curls about the bottom of the mural with the tip dangerously close to its mouth. The dragon's back acts as a dam against a massive flood of pitch black water, frothing and turbulent, and this blackness in turn provides the backdrop for the final piece. A massive bird, presumably Jatayu, but perhaps not, in the midst of having his second wing sliced by a leaping Ravana. The spray of blood is fine and barely visible, but the looks on their faces, both animal and man, are detached disbelief.

Under the gaze of these figures the arms of silent and tacit slaves are weighed down by silver platters covered with high thread count cotton napkins resting under tall thin glasses filled exactly two thirds with Brut Gold champagne, Harlan Estate red wine, or a white from the Grand Cru vineyards. Those with empty platters are taking orders for vodka tonics with two and a half slices of cucumber, one half leaf mint (muddled) and one slice of lemon half zested, old fashioneds with Dalmore or Glenfarclas or Macallan and fingers of Don Julio Real or Casa Herradua or Rey Sol Anejo with a quarter squeezed lime or a full one or half lemon half lime or straight up. The hum of their conversation is like sewage tumbling through derelict pipes in centuries-old cities, coagulating, clogging, then sloshing onward from its own weight pressing into itself, forcing it through lead-laced pipes and dumping into once-fresh rivers and seas. Hands move unnecessary food to mouths that aren't hungry and dentured teeth work brioche and caviar or gravad lax or smoked salmon and goat cheese into a digestible paste that's washed down with cocked eyebrows and a nod regarding a story about a hedge fund or a round of golf with so-and-so prime minister or last week's vacation to the Maldives.

The tittering, chatting and drinking all stop the instant a platter crashes to the floor.

The shattering champagne glasses stranded a dozen hors d'oeuvres between plate and mouth, jokes fluttered like one-winged birds as their punchlines were absent, the trickery of flirting couples talking through plastic surgery evaporated in the burning silence. She had tumbled in the exact center of the ballroom amidst the artificial symmetry of the floor, the lineages of abasement, the unfathomable and unusable wealth.

Everyone stops to stare inward.

Executive Vice President of Operations for Reinventing Energy, a shale oil production and refinery giant in Canada, sat between a Japanese model and a Russian actress, the incident interrupting lies and ushering their hands above the table. Russel Vintin was wearing a black four-button Alexander Arnoso suit with a white shirt and black tie and growing from his wrist was a Harry Winston he told people he bought when he was twenty. A Dalmore decanter rested on the table, reflecting the bright red Shu Uemura lipstick and matching Roberto Cavalli one-piece of the Japanese model, her black hair in a pinned backside that framed one side of her face while revealing the rest. Her mouth slid open in shock, a manicured hand floated to her face, which held the cracked seeds of a smile. Her Russian counterpart leaned forward and took a sip of the Dalmore then licked her lips as the smoky clove fire ran down the inside of her throat and coated her belly, waiting for more. Lurid yellow curls fell over her shoulders like drunk tentacles, she popped her lips and sat back, and her breasts bobbed sickeningly as her matching Cartier necklace and bracelet glistened like cousins of the chandeliers.

A South Korean diplomat, drowning in a deep blue Burberry shawl, shifted the bust of her evening gown, a custom Kate Spade, while everyone glared at the enticing calamity. The dress was black, inlaid with delicate flowers matching the shawl that was draped over her milky shoulders and framed a silver and sapphire Chopard necklace. She sat with fearlessly judgemental eyes, large and dark, matching the figure of a caged minotaur that rested in the center of a thin, braided silver tiara. Her husband smiled slow after deluging himself in a sea of Glenfiddich '37. He silently celebrated the fact that this wasn't his first ball and how he didn't have to catch or cook his own food like his father had. His glass hand was endowed with a gold set of Graff rings, bracelet and cufflinks ordained with circular diamonds. The hiatus in nonchalant bragging with the table of German bankers to his left was welcome and he sat and was drunk and waited for everything to unfold as the silent anticipation built like magma under the remnants of an ancient glacier.

A table of pharmaceutical executives—American, German, Dutch, English—stopped their quarterly earnings gloating to gaze at the flurry of commotion which was now a freakish stillness, a staring contest between a hundred eyes trained inward and a single heavy pair looking at bits of glass shimmering in palms. The American, 52 and looking 30, wearing a three-button charcoal Karl Donoghue with white gold cufflinks, a Chopard LOC Tourbillon on his wrist, grinned. The German, wrapped sharply in an all-black Neil Barrett with a white tie, smelled of Clive Christian and held two fingers of Highland Park halfway to his mouth with a maniacal grin of pity and hunger and happiness smeared across his handsome face which was framed by a fashionable lopsided French hairstyle. The Dutch woman's breasts were barely contained by a deep v-cut shimmering blue Vivienne Westwood dress, her splotchy skin rendered impeccable by an Aveda cream costing $600 an ounce. Her matching watch and bracelet, Mikimoto braided gold, dangled down her wrists as she rested her head in her hands, awaiting what promised to be another fulfillment of divine order with wide, wet eyes. The Englishman, working towards drunk and slightly out of place in a brown double breasted Anderson Shepherd, platinum cufflinks, a pink Austin Reed shirt and red tie, leaned back, his rheumy eyes feverish with a learned lust and palms slick with want. He looked in with everyone else waiting to see who would move first.

Sir Blanchard stared at the heels of her palms and the subtle—yet to the experienced eye, noticeable—creases made from hours of washing dishes in hot water, crashing huge pots against each other, furiously rubbing them with metal mesh scrubbers and industrial soap. He wore a three-button Lloyd Hermes jacket with a red Adolfo shirt and black tie, pink and red wingtip shoes by Ferragamo and a custom gold Rolex. The knob in the middle of his throat bobbed with incessant swallowing. His mistress was barely covered in a sheer Gaultier dress, cinched at the waist, a Van Cleef and Arpels necklace fell down her meek cleavage and ended with a trio of yellow diamonds, as did her Piaget earrings, each of them matching her wine and cigarette stained teeth. Nail polish and lipstick by Essie matched the stones. She cleaned imagined dirt from her cuticle and stared.

The head of an American private military company had deposited himself with his 27-year-old wife before anyone else had arrived and proceeded to become impeccably drunk. He had a finger inside her and was about to manifest the remainder of his destiny when the centerpiece's terminal affliction of chance furnished his caprice with a new victim. He wore a blue single button Berluti jacket, a pale blue Brioni scarf and a white shirt from the same brand. She was held together by a loud Moschino skirt and two gold Buccellati bracelets studded with rubies. She sighed softly as he exited her and noticed the appealing paradox of youthful cheeks and taut, clear skin around the neck compromised by the surprising presence of wrinkles creeping out from the edges of the eyes. She pondered briefly would could force so much worry out of such a young body and was genuinely interested in the causes—she had read somewhere such creases were permanent—but remembered there was more Vieilles Vignes she had to drink, and did so, eyes perusing, waiting.

An immense man from the Congo with rings on every finger of his left hand looked at the shoulders and clicked his teeth in disappointment as his head rocked back and forth like an obsidian pendulum of judgment. A single breasted, double buttoned, deep blue Stefano Ricci jacket rested over a white Prada shirt and red tie. His forehead gleamed but he wasn't sweating so much as exuding the generations of tyranny and massacre he'd risen through. He had seen this posture many times before during war and poaching trips into the bush. Curved back, shoulders leaning forward and folding the chest in, lowered head. He saw this, sat back, and poured himself more scotch. His torrent of bloodthirst weakened to a trickle now that she'd subdued herself rather than snapping like a viper or kicking out like the cornered horse she was. She wasn't as dark as him—so maybe not as strong, he thought—but she still had the color of earned pride in her skin. He passed his raven hand across his brow and cleared his throat quietly. *America,* he thought, *home of the estranged and land of the meek.*

An Italian photographer in a one-piece flower print satin dress was enamored with the wet glass scattered around the human centerpiece and the urge to snap a few shots of this magnificent moment was tempered by the fact her husband had forbidden her from bringing anything save her clutch, condoms, and a sniffer of cocaine. The composition was marvelous, even appetizing, to the right mind: glistening, kaleidoscopic diamonds, unforgettably beautiful and contrasted perfectly by the subject, half-kneeling, half-sitting. A monument to defeat and dejection. On her skin was a slight film of sweat, so with the right angle, her skin would shine just like the diamonds. The photographer licked her lips, took a sip of wine and squeezed her legs together.

"Well," the owner of four South African diamond mines begins, fracturing the silence and bringing to a head the task for the evening. He wears a notched, single breasted three-button Cesare Attolini jacket with an Ozwald Boateng shirt and tie with platinum cufflinks and a silver Rolex. He moves between the tables like an orca, his motions heavy and deliberate. He drags his Rick Owens shoes the final few feet before stopping, his fang-like fingers tucked into his pants. His head cocked, he looks down.

She sighs, a quiet song of pity that is as natural as a gazelle's gasp as her hind legs are shattered with the swipe of a paw, an acceptance of reality and release of life.

He hitches his pants and kneels down, gently brushing away errant strands of hair that came loose in the fall. He wants to see her face.

She doesn't move, keeping her eyes down, looking at

but ignoring the spreading puddle of champagne, a tiny lake filled with tadpoles of glass.

She feels a hand trace around her cheek, glide down her neck and squeeze her shoulder, testing its firmness. She wants to cry but chooses not to even as fingers prod her breasts, her arms are pinched by someone from behind and a third pair of hands press into her supple back. Her cheeks are squeezed and as the exploring, testing, gauging moves from her breasts to her ribs, she slips her palms over her belly, the tears welling but not falling. She knows what she is now.

More hands come to her, chairs slide out, silverware and ice in empty glasses sing a pleasant, empty song as the crowd gathers. Her head is pulled back from behind and hands are running along the muscles above her breasts. Smooth, repulsive fingers grip her thighs. Soon eager and prospective hands are judging every part of her body and her clothes are quickly peeled away as if by deft hunters, exposing every curve and crevice of her save the precious few inches of her lower stomach, still held by her palms.

She is a drop of water in a frothing stream.

She is lifted from the floor but not elevated above the crowd, the hands become more energetic—not quite frantic—but more deliberate in what they grab, and how. Nails dig into either side of her right calf, teeth nibble her muscular buttox, someone smells the cavity of her left hip and flicks their tongue out, tasting her sweat.

The stream is rushing, turbulent and wild, following the only path it knows, following until it throws itself over a cliff, cascading into a terminable waterfall.

Teeth sink into her neck and shoulder and life pours out of her, lapping over faces, gurgling around noses and swallowed down throats.

As the single drop of water falls and nears the abyss, it disintegrates—the fall too high, the speed too great—into an anonymous mist. She lets her hands fall to her sides and whispers: "Isaiah."

The fibers of a calf separate and the extra leverage is

greeted with delight: the muscle is ripped free and eager teeth sink in, chewing loudly. A thigh and buttocks are split with great effort, legs twisted out at unnatural angles and with the loud snap of her pelvis, the ripping begins in earnest and a frenzy is born. Blood sprays from her neck, a cheek is ripped from its home, a breast is chewed noisily, the fatty tissue savored between low grunts. An entire leg is finally twisted off and the fountain of crimson is rhythmic and massive but short lived as a mouth covers the artery and chugs, blood spraying over cheeks and chin and nose. A head is buried in the soft flesh below the ribs and makes impressive progress. An eyeball is patiently extracted, edged out like a precious gem, then examined and polished just as thoroughly before being devoured in a single, ecstasy-filled bite. Calves are to the bone and neck vertebrae are showing when the large intestine is reached, but from opposite sides of the meal. It takes a second to tear out the slippery organ, and the brief tug of war that follows is ended by someone biting it through the center. The mostly digested contents begin to spill out but are slurped up and sucked out like hot porridge on a cold winter Sunday. A fat man leans in and grasps a lung then pulls. He's eventually successful and shuffles to the edge of the frenetic buffet and chews on the rubbery organ, content as an infant with its favorite pacifier. Ribs are cracked open and spread like fleshy wings to reveal the next vital course. The heart is chewed out and trained fingers enter the arteries and twist. The muscle cleanly separates as one can split an orange and spill no juice. A woman tears out the liver and lays the whole thing over her head, rubbing it every which way until someone takes it and slaps her hard and loud across the face. The sound makes a few of the most disgusting and perverted laugh and chortle, blood choking their nostrils and bits of organ shooting from their mouths.

The frenzy is at its peak, but for some reason, from the very center, there is a pause. Mouths and fingers slow as two hands cup the grand prize. Blood drenched hands form a bowl, and at the center is a delicacy so well presented—

droplets of blood glistening, purple and blue veins displaying an immaculate aging process, the bulbous head and the tiny, prawn-like frame—that one would think only a master craftsman could conjure something so beautiful. The fetus is raised high for all to appraise and savor before it is lowered into a mouth, the pop of its soft skull like a grape pressed slowly between teeth. A tiny mist of innards puffs out then quickly dissipates to nothing and the feast resumes.

Bones are split for marrow, cartilage is gnawed unappreciatively and those who began the meal saunter back, content for now, as those on the perimeter slowly filter in to pick at what's left of the vitals. Blood washes over the shattered glass and mixes with the champagne, the pool massive and spreading.

Seats are taken, conversations resumed, wine-stained teeth no more so than before, those buzzed on liquor now drunk with blood. Wristwatches and bracelets are adjusted, thousand dollar bras shuffled a bit to coddle useless breasts, cellphones checked, affairs and trade deals planned with a few taps of a few fingers. The lake of blood in the center of balanced geometric beauty is garish and wild in its uncontrollable ebbs and flows. The tacit slaves walk over it with eyes straight ahead. Their knees and calves tense yet they don't, or can't, change their pace.

Beyond the mahogany doors and through the fabricated bird feeders and fountains, out of the fractured light of the chandeliers, past the erected barriers of life and space, Montgomery clears his throat and stands after stretching his legs out. He walks along the barricade, letting his fingers tap along the tall metal spears, listening to the lotus flower fountains sing a faint song only he is privy to. The main gate is locked and guarded but the gentle light is allowed to spill into the street to illuminate the grit, and him. Guards stare and grip their batons. The man stops and looks. A rat scurries in from the gutter and onto his foot to nibble at his rotting pants. He looks down and gives the rodent a noncommittal shove, shaking it off and continuing his walk through the fingerprint of the city.

*from the top everything seems so
simple.* Uniform. Ubiquitious.

Graveyard

There is no forgiveness when you're at the apex

there is only failure

The scribbled letters were different sizes and the words barely followed the blue lines. *We have her and u wont ever see her alive.* The note was crumpled and there was a thick crease down the center where the note had been tied to a rock, which had landed on Monica's brick patio, interrupting their search. It was the only part she could read before the boulder of panic cracked their smoldering worry into an open flame of panic. The tea party was ruined: two pink chairs upended, a table flipped sending the kettle of imaginary Earl Grey flying, small feet stomping and running, pink silverware and grubby hands flailing.

The rest of the note was almost destroyed amidst the lolling side-ponytails and juice boxes. *Unless u bring too boxes of Oreos UNOPENT to the park behind the big swirly slide.*

The immensity of the task quadrupled when the final line was struggled out by Monica: *And milk. Chocolate A gallon.. Tru Moo.* The final parts were written in haste and mockery.

Moans of despair, pouty faces and clenched fists populated the backyard of 192 Glendale Road in Newton, Massachusetts. Everyone was crushed and everything was awry. Nothing would be the same again. Olivia, the guest of honor, the best dressed, the newest and cleanest of the American Girl dolls, was gone. Stolen. Michelle's eyes followed the ransom note, a most delicate wrecking ball, as it floated from Monica's hands and onto the thick grass. She slumped down and began to shake with quiet, slow sobs. Monica rushed to her with Sarah and Lina following close behind.

Michelle continued to look at the note, suspended by a

147   *which is death.*

few thin blades. Her face contorted into a pink, teary mess.

Four sat, consoling. One stood, brooding.

The speeding train of preadolescent grief was derailed with a single syllable uttered from below long, dark bangs: "No."

The sobbing went silent. They stared, unbelieving.

Sometimes, when engulfed in impossibility, the only option is insanity.

Cameron walked over to the note and picked it up, lips silently rereading the words to herself. *Who?* she thought. *Who would do this for Oreos? Who would demand that much chocolate milk?* Her mind raced through everyone she knew. *Paul had Oreos last week, but he was sharing them. Chris got in trouble for stealing Nicole's animal pen set, but he wasn't smart enough to write like this. Cassandra and Emily, maybe? Michelle did spill water color on her giraffe. It was an accident, but Cassandra was super angry.* The answer came to her slowly. She could see him giving the orders, detailing what to write and reassuring how it'd work. "This is from Anthony," she said, remembering how he got in a fight over a spot in the lunch line. "Bobby's with them too." He was the best writer in fourth grade and loved baseball. *But who was smart enough, quick enough, to actually take Olivia?* "And Saresh. Definitely Saresh."

Four voices started at once and were silenced when Cameron started tearing the note apart, strip by strip. "We know where they are," Cameron began. Michelle blinked and swallowed hard, slowly pushing herself to her feet, the others crouched and still. "We have to take her back," Cameron continued, putting a hand on Michelle's shoulders. "She's yours. She's *ours*." The rest of the girls stood and exchanged glances, knowing what had to be done.

The tea party remains were gathered and rushed inside the quiet, clean house. The remaining dolls were stashed inside and upstairs, locked in Monica's closet. The snacks were stored in the kitchen, a few rogue potato chips crunched loudly, the cupcakes covered.

Monica and Lina's parents were at church, while Cameron, Michelle, and Sarah's were at the water appropriation rally.

Pink shoes, bobbing ponytails, striped dresses, plastic necklaces, and elastic bracelets marched down the street towards conflict and reclamation.

A long, curving left turn brought them on to the same street as the enemy base. Four bicycles, a football, a plastic bat, three plastic baseballs and two backpacks lay on the grass in front of a massive sycamore tree. The fort was behind the tree: sticks and plywood, cardboard and a broken recycling bin patched together to form a hut. The squad approached the tree slowly, trying to make sense of the heightened mumbling they heard.

Michelle held the cupcakes, everyone else their fists. They stopped in the middle of the boys' mess, about twenty feet from the tree.

Cameron picked up a plastic baseball and lofted it high and long, the arc splendid, her aim accurate. An innocent *dink* off a piece of plastic roof did nothing to quell the murmurs or get anyone's attention. She wet her lips and looked around. Near one of the bikes was a rock slightly smaller than her fist. Cameron walked over.

The rock crashed through a piece of cardboard and Cameron smiled, the other girls took a half step back. Shouting, a muffled yell—crying?—and finally the boys rounded the tree.

The girls looked at each other. They outnumbered the boys, but they had two allies the girls lacked: size and malice.

Cameron stared at Anthony. Then at each of them in turn: Kevin, the smallest, glasses, black hair like hers, grubby khaki shorts and a navy blue shirt. Saresh, bushy black hair, massive brown eyes, red sweat pants and a dirty white shirt. Bobby, faded New York Yankees shirt, gray shoes that used to be white, and blonde crew cut. He tried to stand tall and covered his right hand with his left, face taut, anticipating.

"Give her back," Cameron demanded.

"You know what we want," Anthony asserted.

Cameron looked at Michelle and they nodded at each other. Cameron saw a face not unlike the one painted on the dolls.

"Show us first," Cameron ordered, staring at Anthony.

"Doesn't look like you have everything you need..." Anthony retorted, tilting his head and looking at the plastic box.

"We have it all. We want to know she's safe. Show us she's okay, and you get the first half. When you hand her over, you'll get the rest."

Anthony took a half step back and sniffed the air, looking for weakness in Cam's words and finding none. He looked at Kevin and mumbled something. Kevin took his time in complying, but left and returned with Olivia.

Michelle beamed and almost dropped the cupcakes. "Not yet, they can still hurt her," Cameron whispered, but she could see the anxiety welling up in Michelle, any more and the geyser would erupt. Michelle nudged the plastic container away from herself, shaking her head. Cameron looked into the wide, watery eyes and understood. She took the cupcakes and turned around.

Olivia was fine—her clothes were dirty, hair scraggly and they'd drawn all over her arms and face with green and brown marker, but she was still intact, still alive.

Cameron walked slowly toward the boys, cupcakes first, and stopped a few feet in front of Anthony. He got on his tip toes and peered through the opaque plastic. "*Those* aren't Oreos—" slapping the container from the bottom and into the air, sending pastries flying and girls screaming. The boys' eyes widened with surprise then their mouths dropped in shock when he pushed Cameron.

She fell hard on both elbows. The cupcakes were strewn to her left, most falling frosting first, completely ruined.

"You *know* what we *wanted*—" Anthony jeered, stepping forward, but Cameron didn't see this. She saw Kevin's arms above his head throwing Olivia. The wingless beauty who'd suffered so much was staged to endure another chap-

J. Gray

ter of grief. Michelle's scream ignited a primal fire, and before Olivia landed softly in the grass, there was a cupcake in Cameron's hand.

The frosted end exploded into Anthony's eye and the delicious, untasted sweetness smeared over his face. He barely had time to shout as Cameron's fist smashed his cheek and robbed him of sight from his other eye. Michelle's voice crescendoed and Cameron's head rocked back with a punch from Saresh that sent her sprawling. Lying on the grass, heart racing, face pounding, Cameron felt a flush of victory sweep her as she saw tears stream down Anthony's face as he screamed "*You*—"

"—*bitch! Wake the fuck up!*" The cold water erases the green grass, the fear in Michelle's voice, the unbelieving anger in Anthony's face and any semblance of victory.

I awake to chains and painful light. I'm hanging against a wall by my wrists, with my ankles locked, forcing my legs together. It's hard to breathe. I drag my sandy tongue over my wet chin and lips. I've never known a thirst like this. I blink, trying to see.

White magma pours from a door in front of me and into my skull. I jerk my head to the left, someone's there, but the pain in my neck grays my vision and my knees weaken. My head is pulled back, I feel my eyes melt and collect into pools at the base of my spine as my neck splinters and frays like an old burnt rope. Something cold and wet and wonderful is forced into my mouth. I bite and suck and swallow. I swallow again, sigh, swallow a third time and a palm crashes into my face, knocking my face against the wall and the wet cloth from my mouth. I squeeze my eyes shut but the light pierces through the pathetic shield of flesh. Shadows form and disappear on the walls of my eyelids. I try to stand, then slump down. My wrists are burning. Hands lift me up and push me against the wall. The torrent of light is obscured by a thin frame.

"You will die here," a voice of ice begins, "and everything you love will crumble while you bleed." The hands drop me but my knees don't buckle. My head is jerked forward by vice grips on my skull and light frames a profile of oblivion. "Why?" The syllable reeks of malice and curiosity. "Why do you even bother?"

I try to beg for water but a soundless click is all my throat produces. My hair is released and I'm punched in the stomach and slapped in the face. I try to breathe through the pain and fail, dry heaving and coughing. "Your friends were weak," the profile says, walking away, the stabbing light growing larger as her shape shrinks. The door swings, a latch lands home and all is black.

It's raining. It's still dark and it's raining. It falls down my back, soaks my hair and runs into my nose and mouth. In the darkness I can move my head enough to tell it's from a spigot in the ceiling. I'm cold and alive. I greedily swing my tongue around, lapping up as much as I can, stretching my jaws to their limits. The water runs down my back and thighs, it drips from my hair. Each drop that hits the floor mocks my thirst.

Time passes. I'm dry. A door opens and the needles are back in my eyes stitching patches of insanity onto my mind. The door is closed but not all the way, and the shadows this time are slow, the profile different. Someone sits in front of me. I grunt and manage an audible click amidst the rocks in my throat when a hand touches my head, cooing to me, telling me to not try, to rest, apologizing for the shackles and someone named Kimmy. The touch is a caress, and after the shackle's embrace, brings unbidden tears to my eyes.

My cheeks are in palms that feel like an endless bed of flower petals. There's fire running up my wrists and legs and tears down my face. With a gentle squeeze, thumbs caress my closed, wet eyelids. My head's cradled and tilted from side to side with gentle strength, and the pain in my neck makes me sweat. She breathes close to me. She's clean, she's soft, she's kind. My head keeps moving and my throat rattles, pleading for water and freedom. "I know it hurts," she whispers, sliding her wrists down my cheeks and around my neck. "I'll get you what you need." Her wrists are punctuated with raised, smooth scars. Her thumbs rest along my jaw and her palms against my throat. She stays like this for a while.

"I'm here because I have to be," she finally whispers, breathing slowly, never letting go of my face. Her fingers begin to sweat as they grip. "Just like you." Her aroma of cleanliness morphs into a putrid stench and I try to pull away from her, to get away from her washed hair, nourished skin and lack of filth, but her hands tighten. "Please," she asks and means it, pressing into my neck. Panic shortens my breaths. "It doesn't have to be hard, it doesn't have to hurt. The pain," she reveals her words slowly like a prophet. "Is a choice."

I swallow painfully, loudly, and think about my breathing. "You always have a choice, and you've been brought here to make one. Now," She speaks slowly and with immense conviction as she releases my neck. The weight of my head is stunning and I gasp as my muscles struggle. "When you got to the Dozers, how many cars and how many people were you with?"

The needle of light gives her face a shape and texture: soft curves and beautiful complexion. It brings me back to the raspy-voiced girl with the shaved head and the tattoo. My mind wanders to the flirting, the kissing, the playing that became choking and this woman who smells of pristine filth is walking away. The door creaks open, and I cough: "Three."

She stops, the light making me squint, the pain drowning my thirst.

"Three cars." She turns back, looks at me, but I can see only light and dark, her humanoid silhouette and the blinding hallway. "Fifteen of us."

She leans the door almost closed and walks back to me, taking something from her pocket. She kneels down in front of me and my ankles are free. I'm moving and flexing my knees, rotating each foot in turn. She leaves the room for what feels like a few minutes and returns with a plastic cup of water that she brings to my mouth. My heart races and my breathing is ragged as I finish. The water is the most delicious thing I've ever tasted until there's a small piece of chocolate in my mouth. Pain and disbelief disappear in sweetness and relief. The door clanks shut and I'm alone, the chocolate disappearing in my mouth.

There's nothing to hear and nothing to see. There is only silence and darkness. The water's gone and the lingering sweetness on my tongue mocks my hunger. My wrists throb in the shackles, they're raw and getting worse. I try to remember what happened, when and with who, but there's a wall of fog between me and my memories, like the door blocking the light from the hallway.

The door slams open, the light crushes my attempts to remember and a rush of footsteps ends with something crashing into my face.

"She won't get away with shit like that again," a fierce whisper that's followed by the door slamming shut, the gentle darkness, and fresh bouts of pain. The ringing in my ears makes shapes dance in front of my eyes.

I think I sleep. I can barely move. Something like hours pass when the door opens and is leaned to. Slow feet work their way forward and something about apologies is muttered as the shape sits down a few feet in front of me. She sets a ring of keys and a tray down in front of her. "It's a shame some people can't be more . . ." I can hear he lick her lips with a moist tongue, thinking. "Civil." She sighs and I feel her gaze. "Time for a few more choices."

I try to look at her but can't make out any features of her face or what's on the tray. She waits and I think about the water and the chocolate. I lick my lips with a thick tongue. I inhale and she stands, tells me to open my mouth. I eventually oblige and something cold and sweet and juicy is on my tongue and she orders me to chew. I would have collapsed if not for the chains. It's a slice of an orange. I chew slowly and deliberately. I encounter a seed and chew through it, and do the same with the second, which is dry and bitter. There's enough juice left to mask the synthetic taste.

After a few minutes she brings more water to my

mouth. The shape of her hand, her neck and her chin become more defined. I can see the outline of the walls, the corners. She's framed by a thin rectangle of light, the tiniest fractions of freedom breaking through the edges of the door. I see this and am filled with an incredible fear.

A knot forms in my stomach like a tremor before an earthquake. My knees buckle and my arms shake with the weight of my body. My breathing is erratic and I start sweating and grunting, trying hide my weakness but failing. My knees are shaking and bombs are going off inside of me, the explosions low and slow forming like they're underwater. I didn't realize she'd been speaking, but I latch on to the tail end of a sentence.

"... that to the water supplies, it was only a few months before the first cases of really bad dysmeno started cropping up. We have stuff to take care of it here, thankfully. It'd be so hard to get anything done without it." I hear a small sigh of pity and concern when I feel it dripping down my leg. "You've got the menorra too? No wonder you're so upset. Not to mention running around with *those* people. Don't worry," she says, standing and walking away. "We have everything you need to be everything you want." There's a flash as she exits and a rush of cramps and I almost pass out.

The blood is spreading between my thighs and I'm needlessly embarrassed. I feel my face reddening and wonder how long this one will last. Each one previous had been getting longer and longer, the pain slowly escalating like a helium filled balloon. Soon I'd either pop or continue to deflate until everything inside me was empty and shrivelled. I concentrate on my breathing.

An argument starts in the hallway, but it's hushed and far from the door. It becomes tense, almost shouting, the exchanges long and measured. There are footsteps clacking down the hallway, and the argument is completed with a "Fine, fuck you." After a shape walks past and right before a door to the left is slammed: "You can clean up that pile of shit in 307."

I hear low muttering and slow footsteps, then the door opens. I squirm and try to move my head away but my neck is too stiff. Everything in my body is screaming and I can feel the precipice approaching after which are only insanity and death. "We're better at giving the migraines than stopping them. The light will hurt for a while, but your muscles will loosen up pretty soon."

I look at her head and can't see a face, only a black figure with a soothing liquid voice. She brings her hand to my mouth with something in her fingers. I clench my lips shut.

"Not everyone here is out to hurt you, you know," she says patiently. "I know what it feels like out there. Your life doesn't have to be that way. There are ways out," she brings her hand up again and I look at her, the void of her face dissipating as the whites of her eyes, a dark line of her lips and a blurred oval of a head materialize. I stand there bleeding, a small pool collecting at my ankles. She looks down and lets loose another quick sigh. "Here," she insists, putting two pills in my mouth. She leaves the room and I bite down as the light strikes me, the bitterness a weak distraction.

"Kimmy didn't start out like us," she says, giving me water. "She was born into this. Always having, never wanting. That's why she's like that." There's a hand on my lower stomach. "I know what it's like." Through the darkness that separates us she stares into my eyes and gives her sermon. "To struggle, to fight, to lie, to kill, suffering every single day, just to survive for another day of despair." She comes closer and her smell fills my nostrils, dousing me with envy and nausea. "There's a way. There's a way out of everything," Our noses are almost touching. "But we can't get there alone." She's cupping my face again and for the first time my fear is gone. My knees are calm and the light crescendos at the top of her head, a star-like halo that hides her face.

"You give me answers, I give you comfort," she steps away. She pulls a knife from a sheath behind her back. It's cold against my thigh.

I swallow and the click in my throat echoes in the cell.

"I want to help you," the serrated edge dragging down the inside of my thigh. "And I will." It moves back up and slips through the front of my soaked underwear and is tilted away from me. She pulls, snapping the front open.

"But I still have a job to do." She inches from my face she guides the knife home and takes keys from her pocket.

She unlocks my right wrist and I twist it around, making sure it's okay. She moves to unlock the other when I stab her in the eye with all five fingers in a tight, pointed beak. I feel something pop.

She stumbles back, doubled over, holding her face. Before she can grab her knife I launch myself up—pulling with my trapped left wrist—I wrap my calves around her neck and squeeze. I link my ankles for more leverage as my body screams in pain. She's twisting, gurgling, arms flailing before finally managing to get her knife out. I rub my knees back and forth and feel pieces of her throat come loose. She cuts at my legs, a few long slices but no stabs, and she's panicking. Her knees begin to fail and she squirms, twitches for a few seconds then stops.

I use my toes to search for the keys. I unlock myself and take her knife. As soon as I'm in the hallway the light explodes into my eyes and brings me to my knees.

The dimness of the cell seems like a refuge.

I crouch down and throw my hands over my eyes, knowing there's someone else not far, assuming they've seen everything, hoping they're not on their way. I look both ways down the hallway and see two exits on either end with doors along both walls.

I squint and see 307 to my left. The first few keys fail but the fourth and the door yields and the darkness is inviting. The familiar shape I see on the floor mutes the pain, my feet carry me in, and then I see what's left of his face.

I am lost. My knees surrender and I'm holding his bloody head, brushing away matted hair and crying. I fold myself over him and fight the violent sobs, breathing loudly. I think about the last moment of peace, just before we walked into Burc's room, wishing I kissed him. My tears have cleaned a spot on his cheek, I bring my lips to it and my hands are steel around his skull. My breathing is quick and shallow and the tides of panic are seeping into my chest. Still gripping him, I count. In for 3 seconds, hold for 3 seconds, out for 3 seconds. I can eventually feel my hands again. I put them on my knees and focus on the first thing that will keep me alive: standing.

The hallway is long and heavy with him. To the left, a door. To the right, the same, only farther. I choose left and sprint to the end of the hallway. Between breaths I hear a clang and see the latch on the door turning. I run for the hinges, just as the door opens, keeps opening, I'm on my tip toes with my back against the wall not breathing, door inching closer and closer pressing my breasts flat against me, when it finally begins to recede. The guard walks with her gun drawn, silent and alert. My hand sweats around the knife. His door is barely open. My face is hot and panic fresh in my chest.

The door she came through closes loudly and I move from the wall. She stops, speaks into a radio and doesn't move. She speaks again and waits, curses, taking small steps. Pistol in hand, nightstick, 2 extra clips, flashlight on her belt. I can't see what's attached to the front. I walk in step with her, delicately folding the outside of my foot inward, my back is straight and I breathe deep with my belly, quietly. She reaches the door and prepares herself, pistol raised.

She jumps around the door, aiming the firearm and I plant my left foot while kicking my right at the door. It smashes into her and she's off-balance and I'm behind her in two steps, folding her right knee with a kick and stabbing down into her neck. It opens with vast bursts of blood. She vaults backwards, almost topples then kicks her legs out planting both of us on my back. All breath explodes from my lungs but my grip remains. She rolls on her sides and throws elbows like she's trained but none of them land. Her strength rushes out of her like water off a cliff.

Her belt doesn't fit. I carry a pistol in my right hand, keys hooked on my pinky, the flashlight and knife in my left. The stairway is brightly lit so I crouch in the corner until the pain fades. Looks down and up are identical: endless stairs.

I look back in the dimmer hallway, at all the other cells, each potentially holding someone that was almost a friend. I think about hauling the guard's body into the cell, but can't handle looking at him again. I look down and wonder what answers I'll find if I descend. I load a round in the chamber and begin climbing.

I walk carefully with my pistol up and ears open. None of the keys work on the first door, but the second yields. I move the latch inch by inch and with agonizing patience I lean into the door and moonlight spills out, forcing me to pause. Camping trips in Maine, swimming in Clary Lake, ham and swiss sandwiches, applesauce, our tree house just outside Jefferson that Grandpa built. I swallow and lunge inside to a wall of monitors. The grainy colors are constellations of movement that all at once confuse me. The hum of their life is unnatural, belying all the people I see.

I breathe and focus on one monitor at a time: a person is struggling to push a huge container of white powder, another row is people tipping similar containers into a huge, vibrating contraption, others attending a series of huge, rapidly spinning machines. Those not watching the spin are tipping containers through open doors. Another row of monitors show people using large scoops to transfer white tablets to a slowly rotating orange chamber. Yet another row is filled with people standing, their backs to the camera—a yellow blur of plastic tubes moving in from of them.

It's all a flurry of motion, a coordinated dance I don't understand. On the far right, three columns of utter stillness and inviting darkness reside on the monitors. I step closer and see that all these show only one person each—not shoveling, checking, pushing, or locking—all of the monitors still or completely empty. Each square a beacon of solitude—save one. Light spills in and Stephan's body casts a shadow that covers the whole room.

There's a row of monitors showing hallways. One of them shows the guard's body and her blood. That stillness is surrounded by a dance of constant motion. I look down and breathe slow. The pistol and knife are heavy. The room is dirty and dark but still lighter than the cell. I sit and try to ignore the dance on the monitors by remembering what happened at the Dozers'. Glimpses of the car ride and white lines on a mirror are all that I can find. My head is pounding. The flashlight, shining on the ceiling, looks like a giant and unreachable star.

Adrenaline from the guard and the stairs fades, my wrists and ankles are sore and my throat throbs in time with my pulse. I can feel cuts and bruises all over my cheeks and head. I try to run my hand through my hair but it's matted with sweat and blood. I'm hungry but not starving, I couldn't have been out for more than 8 hours. I release the magazine and count. Fifteen with one in the chamber.

I turn and look at the monitors. I see thirty people working, and that's just what the cameras are on. These aren't the ones I need. They know nothing. Innocent blood is useless. I see the choreography of the monitors broken by a group of people sprinting down a white hallway, all of them wearing helmets and carrying rifles.

In the stairwell I pause. I look up at unimagined heights and below to familiar struggle.

Stephan's gone. Kevin won't make it. Bianca and Robert—"they never had it in them," I mutter to myself. Down the stairs is the neverending fight. One day to the next. To the next. To the next. I look up and the dim light is enough to make me squint.

I snort back the mouthy bile of tears and spit it down the shaft, taking the stairs up, two at a time.

The next two flights have no doors. The one after does but the latch is jammed. There's a small opaque window and I hear someone opening the door. I dash up the stairs but halfway up the next flight is a brick wall. It's blocked. Entirely.

If anyone walks over just a few feet from the door, they'll see me. The door's innards click and I can see it start to move. The blocked noise of vast machinery from beyond the door crashes into the hallway and I try to slow my breathing, knowing they're coming, my back against the blockade. The door starts to close, the noise recedes, and they begin to talk fast. There's two of them.

"Prop it—don't forget!" Sounds younger, an edge to his voice, high but with a roughness to it. The other sighs— sounds like he's sitting down. "We only have three minutes, it's not like—"

"Relax," he's older, sounds small, speaks with a calmness and a deep rasp. "They barely give a shit about the mycin line." A lighter kicks into life and there's a pause. "The prazos have guards *at their backs,*" the older one coughed with the last three words.

"That's, well," another flick of the lighter. Inhale, exhale. "You know." A small cough.

I sit quietly against the wall: if I take two steps to my left, I'd be looking down a flight of stairs right at them. I sit and think, ignoring their conversation, the click of the lighter punctuating whose turn it was to speak. A small cramp wracks my body and plants itself like an immoveable tornado and the only thing I can think of is stomping boots and rifles. The tides of panic continue to rise but the pain pushes me into action.

I run my hands between my legs, scooping into myself and spreading the warmth along my thighs. I press the blood between my fingers and my hands. I put the knife and keys behind me, keeping the pistol closer, everything bloody like a violently birthed infant.

I focus on my breathing, making it faster, inserting sobs that escalate from whimpers to heavy groans.

The lighter stops hopping between them and a hushed exchange tells me they've heard. I continue, my wrists behind my bent knees, hiding the deep red grooves from the chains. I see a head poke above the top stair then back down. Loud whispers shoot back and forth.

"My baby," I croak in between sobs, and the whispers stop. The same head pops up and stays. It comes closer, step by step, revealing shoulders and a chest, palms up and facing me. I sit and sob.

"Hey, hey, it's okay." The final few stairs are mounted slowly and the rasp is trying to sound gentle. "Look, what—" The voice is still a few feet away when I look up, presenting a battered face. "It's okay," it's a woman, I notice as her breath hitches. Her face is ancient with stress and disease and her voice is gravel. "Do you remember what happened? Did they give you the IV? Or the pills?" She asks after a moment, kneeling down and glancing backward.

"They," I point up through shaky breaths, "took him. I screamed and I fought—"

"Oh honey," she cooes, shuffling forward, "you never fight—" my left hand grips her throat as my right points the pistol at the young one frozen on the stairs. She struggles but I pull her down, squeeze once as hard as I can and feel something crack then slam my elbow in the back of her head. The moment before my thighs close around her neck, she chokes out words I can't understand.

I stare at the young one. "Don't move when I tell you, you die. Move when I don't tell you, you die." His lips are cracked, his eyes are glazed, he holds a burnt lightbulb and a lighter.

The woman struggles between my legs and I kick my ankles out and fall, her face hitting with a crunch before my knees do.

I look at the other one. "Walk slowly up the stairs."
Nothing.

I cock the hammer and he drops the lightbulb. It shatters and I almost pull the trigger.

He's just a boy. The gnarled skin makes it hard to tell how old, but he's still a boy. He looks at the twitching woman and tears well up and I start to lose my patience.

I stand and my knees pop. He jumps. "Walk up here

and take her suit off."

His lips move but make no sound as he begins with the hood. Front zipper, peeling it down the shoulders, hips, legs, feet. "Sit and face the corner." He does.

"What do you do here?" I ask, pulling zippers on my thighs and chest.

His lips pantomime but finally work. My palms are starting to sweat. "I'm Po. We," he stammers, "I, I'm a dryer."

"What do you dry?" He turns and gives me a confused look. "Clothes? Food? Shit?"

He stammers more, then starts. "It's, I dunno, it's—it comes in huge white clumps, kinda like clay. I dunno what it is," he trails off, searching for words.

"What color is it?"

"Starts kinda gray, mostly white, ends as really bright white. Perfect white."

"How do you dry it?"

He rocks back and forth slightly, gathering his thoughts. "We take a clump and press it flat," he's using his hands, demonstrating, starting to shake a little bit. "Heat that. Cut that after eight minutes. Take separate pieces to rollers, roll them flat. They're usually all cracked up. Take those separate chunks to the sifters." He clears his throat, has a small coughing fit. "We heat and shake, heat and shake, heat and shake until there's no clumps and it's all powder, then it's off to the molds." With nothing to explain his hands linger in the air. His eyes come to mine like a dog waiting for a command.

"Is this the only exit?" I nod toward the door he came out of and he shakes his head. "How many people watch you?" His breath hitches and his eyes wander for a second, then he holds up one finger.

"Stand up." He does." We're going to walk back in. If you do anything I don't like, I'll shoot you in the hip," I point the barrel where the bullet will puncture his pelvis. "And you'll never walk again. Ever. You go first." I put my back against the wall and he starts and stops a few times then rubs his face and takes his necessary steps.

He opens the door. Everything is moving and bright and my eyes are searing but I keep the pistol behind me and the knife pressed against his back. I can barely make out any shapes, suddenly then there are voices yelling over the cacophony of the machines.

Shouting.

All I see is white pain then someone's grabbing my left shoulder, yelling. I step in, spin and cock my left arm, the butt of the pistol smashes into a crotch.

More yelling, footsteps, rushing, I'm pushed and my back's against a wall. The light is tearing itself apart and I begin to see. People are running to the door I just entered. I can see legs, arms, all pumping, all frantic.

My left knee explodes in pain and I'm on the ground, kicked in the head, swimming in gray, kicked in the stomach and unable to breathe. A boot is on my pistol hand and I don't know where the knife is when the shape beating me is toppled to the ground: two people in white suits like mine were running and smashed into him. There's shouting and scrambling, the whirr of the machines continues.

I lean forward, there's a tangle of light and dark limbs. The light is needles in my eyes. I lift my pistol and pull the trigger three times at the darker shape. I get to my knees with a chest full of concrete and now people are screaming. The man who grabbed me, the one whose testicles I decimated, is barely on his feet when I shoot him in the knee.

We're both kneeling, his face tangled in pain and disbelief. I open his face with two rounds. He topples over and the last person in white runs out and the door closes, leaving me with two dead, adjusting to the light.

Colors return, my breathing calms, I can feel the sweat on my face and the dull ache in the pit of my stomach. My ears are ringing from the shots, a high whine.

Two bodies. Six rounds. Careless waste.

My eyes adjust fully and the pain's still there, but now only a dull ache. I search the bodies. Both have expandable batons, key cards with names and magnetic strips. One has a ring of keys, the other a candy bar.

I take the cards, keys, a long baton and eat the stick of nuts and synthetic sugar. I leave the knife. Baton and pistol in hand, I walk to the far door, scanning left and right, listening for movement or an alarm.

There's mold in the corners of the room, rust on the door hinges and the bottom of the massive conveyor belt that won't quit running. The doors are huge and locked with no keyhole. I place one of the key cards on a pad above the the knob. It beeps and a digital keypad reveals itself. I grit my teeth and look around.

The conveyor belt whirls along carrying white powder. I follow it through the room, each corner a vibrating mesh, shaking the powder finer and finer. The belt leads through a wall and there's a doorway covered in plastic flaps to the left of the belt. I drop to a crouch and hold the pistol out, moving slowly. The sound of the shots would have carried through the opaque, dirty plastic. My palms sweat as I lean over the opening in the wall, listening through the loud machines.

It's an ambush. They're waiting for me. I step back inside. I roll one of the bins in front of the door and drag one of the bodies over, folding limbs around wheels. My blood mixes with theirs. I do the same with the sealed door.

My back's against the wall, the plastic flaps to my left. I'm adjusting my grip on the pistol, licking my lips and tasting sweat, anticipating blood and chaos when the plastic flutters beside me.

An unsteady pistol, the same Glock 20 as mine, presents itself, followed slowly by fingers, a wrist, a forearm. I smash the elbow with my baton and lean forward and pull down.

The screams are the worst I've ever heard. The elbow is shattered and the arm is twisted in strange ways. My left hand brings the baton into the flesh between neck and shoulder. I swing three more times and soon there's only twitching.

He's wearing the same dark blue as the other guards. His uniform's more loose, he's swimming in the pants and the whole thing is barely hanging onto his shoulders. Sweat or tears or both mix with the blood that falls from the skull. The skin is dirty but smooth, never marred by a razor. I take the magazine from his pistol, check for a round in the chamber and don't find one. The safety was still on. The pockets are empty.

I swallow the surge of guilt and breathe it into submission.

Peering through the overlaid flaps is impossible. I crouch down against the wall again. There's blood all over the machinery. I lift the closest flap to look past the edge of the wall when the power's cut from the conveyor belt and the hum of electricity evaporates from the air. The belt itself bumbles on for a second under it's own weight, then the silence is again upon me. The lights live.

My breathing sounds like the roaring of a massive blaze. My gut does a somersault and a low, unintentional groan interrupts the flames. I can feel myself dripping slowly down my thighs and buttocks. I'm sweating, shaking, all I can see is Stephan's chest and neck, feel his hands on the sides of my head, instructing me to breathe and count. Breathe and count. Breathe and count. The cramp passes as I look up at his blue, bruised face. Twin rivers of dried blood spill from his nose and over his lips.

I blink his face and my tears away, pushing the watery images into nothingness with the heels of my palms. I wipe my hands on the suit but it absorbs nothing. I blow gently to dry them, grip the baton and pistol, stand.

Slowly, I separate two of the flaps with the baton. I plunge through and raise my pistol to emptiness and something smashes into my wrist from above. Before I can scream or swing I'm hit between the eyes and everything goes dark.

*   *   *

I'm being dragged through a hallway with a clean floor and bright lights that bring the daggers back into my eyes.

Even with them closed tight the pain shortens my breath. The arms pulling me are strong and show no sign of slowing down. I can feel dried blood on my face and my fingers quiver when I try to make fists. My knees and ankles are bound together. The air smells clean and their footsteps echo loudly in my ears. I sniff loudly through my nose, pull my head up and clear my throat. I try to look up and see their faces, but fail. I breathe slowly, remembering what happened since the cell and searching for what happened before. The wall of fog has dissipated some and the throbbing in my head has calmed, but both are still there.

Chains. Thirst. Darkness. A soft voice I strangled. Stephan. The woman and the boy. They're making something here. But what? How many of them survived that escape? Why were they trying to escape? The monitors—were they for the entire building? Where are they taking me?

My mind was sharpening and the questions were mounting when I was dropped in front of a windowless door with an ordinary steel knob. The man to my right turns and pushes the door in, then steps back. The room is bright and I put my hands in front of my face.

There's a foot in the small of my back and it's shoving me through the doorway. "Here you are Miss Timmins." I've never known brightness or torment like this, and even with my palms digging into my sockets, the light still seeps in, unstoppable.

"When you've been living in the shadows of ignorance, the light of reality is a painful thing to be exposed to." Her voice is slow and mellow, reminding me of my grandmother. I'm sweating and my breathing is fast, I'm doubled over and still on my knees. "Slowly," she coos, as if speaking to a thirsty toddler trying to suck down too much water.

She waits and I suffer.

The white rings of pain leaking through the edges of my palms finally lose their edge. I pull my head from the floor and away from the safety of the darkness in my hands. My head just off the floor, my eyes shut tight, the pain recedes and my mind begins to clear like a sunrise melting away a morning fog.

"Hmm," she hums, and I can hear the smile on her face. "See? You're almost out of the shadows, but I still see you have half a foot in the cave. Take your time. There's some water here when you're ready."

I blink a few times and look around without raising my head. There's only one door. The two men behind me. A desk and a chair in front of me, a long table to the far left with about a dozen mismatched chairs around it, all empty. Boxes are stacked everywhere and are falling apart. No sign of windows. The hum of electrical devices is loud—computers, monitors, probably both. I sit up straight and the last vestiges of pain melt from my eyes when I see her face.

The first thing I notice is how beautiful she is. Her hair is in a tight bun, not a strand out of place, her brown cheeks taut and skin clear from blemishes or dirt, her lips pink and hydrated, eyes blue like oceans of the past. The next thing I notice is how she's looking at me. Completely void of contempt or disdain. She's patiently sitting, waiting for me to acclimate to this new environment, to sit up in the light.

The walls are shedding paint. She widens her eyes and uses her flawless face to nod at the chair sitting across from her, asking me to sit.

I pull, slide and half-crawl to the chair with her watching. Halfway there, with her eyes still on me, the joy of her sudden beauty disappears as I remember where I am, who she is, and the two men at the door. The fury builds when I see the chair is far enough away so that she can see the awkward process of me crawling into the chair, trying to prevent it from tipping. She wants to see me struggle, and she does. My pride is betrayed by my red cheeks. When I'm finally sitting I realize we're both the exact same height and I'm staring directly into her eyes. I blink away an image of Stephan's battered head, lick my lips, and slow my breathing.

"So," she begins.

"So," I respond.

"Here you are."

"Here I am."

She smiles and tilts her head. "It's always intriguing. The arrogance of those who don't know they're defeated. Moreover, it's," she searches for the right word, looking at her desk, then finally into my eyes. "Inspiring."

"I'm glad I can," I lick my lips, struggling to not look at the glass and pitcher of water, "provide something for you."

She shares a bored smile. "Sarcasm is a tool for the weak to sound strong, and I know you're not weak Cameron." The sound of my name through her lips is disarming, and I'm back in Maine again, listening to Grandma's encouraging words as I carry a two liter jug of juice to the picnic blanket, telling me how strong I am. "Stephan, though, he wasn't very—"

"*Don't you—*" I barely lean forward and the two men are behind me, pinning my shoulders back.

"Tch—tch—tch," she says, cutting me off with a wave of her hand, and for some reason the gesture stops me cold. "It's just a statement of fact. Like the sun is hot or the air is dirty. He had a bad heart and a drinking problem. We have the medicine for the heart condition, but," she shakes her head. "For us to invest in someone, for us to take the risk of using what we make here on someone who couldn't earn us a net gain, well, that's simply a bad investment."

"And just just what the fuck do you consider your *business?*"

"Survival." She lets the word hang like an anchor. "And what we invest in? He wouldn't be strong enough for it."

My nostrils are flaring but I swallow my fury and ask the question she wants to hear. "For *it?* For survival?" My anger is diffused with my own questions and her voice is a dam to the river of my own thoughts. She exudes a command as if she were bred for it.

"Do you love your friends?" *What friends? After what happened at the Dozers'? After Burc's run? There's no one I can call that.* "Do you want to go back to them?" She pauses, waiting for my answer. I look at her in silence. *Is Kevin dead or just crippled? Are the fridges on Pleasant Street fixed? Burc must have flipped, so did anyone sack him?* "Do you want to return to those unstable, addicted, sick people who leech off your dedication to them, providing you with nothing but injury and anxiety?"

Her question blocks out my own. After a few minutes I answer slowly in a voice with no depth. "They'd die for me, just as I would for them. You have no idea what it's like out there, the things we do for what we need, what we do to keep ourselves and the people we love alive." I stop myself, not wanting to give her too much. "There's nothing we wouldn't sacrifice for each other."

"I'm asking a simple question, Cameron," she says, folding her hands in front of her, elbows on the desk, not annoyed, but carrying on as if handling a student unable to grasp a simple concept.

I stare at her in silence. After a minute she opens her hands, palms up, and shrugs at me, waiting. She pours me some water and slides it across the desk. I take my time and actually think about the question, finally saying: "Yes."

She sighs, shakes her head and I see something leave her eyes as they trail across her desk. "It's too bad you were on the wrong side when the lines were drawn. You could have easily made the cut," she says, leaning forward. "But now," she sighs, "now you're going to die like the rest of your ignorant, unfortunate friends. You're going to die disappointed. Even if you do survive the next year, and your medical issues lessen or you steal enough medicine, you will be dying, if not dead." She spoke with unwavering confidence. Doubting her would be like questioning whether the sun would rise. "Your mind will be riddled with despair." Her jaw muscles tighten and she speaks with slow disappointment. "What you could have been a part of," she looks me in the eye and shakes her head, I'm uncomfortable with her sincerity. "Now, you're going to die with a hollowness devouring you. A feeling of it wasn't *enough*, it was *never* enough, *all* you did, how *you* were never enough, no matter what miracles you worked and temporary smiles you sewed, it never mattered. You still always had to struggle just to avoid complete failure. There was never a victory, never success, never an end, and your noble actions will mean nothing and you'll die in agonizing grief because you'll never be the hero. You will fail. No one will remember you, and you'll die as a pebble amongst mountains." She sighs and wipes a bead of sweat from her temple and waits, looking high over my head.

Burc's speech comes rushing through the fog with immense clarity. The breath of confidence that swept through us as he spoke and the sense of oneness as we trotted out to the cars feels fake, like a plastic sheen. What feels real is the sick old man clinging to life anyway he can. The grime that envelops us all, the sickness and hunger that bind us. As I look at her healthy face I can't help but wonder how all this came to be.

"I could have made the cut for what?"

She stares at me and I look down, not seeing the floor.

"Your dedication to the scum you call friends is outdated and is the end of you. This dedication to the familiar is misplaced. For this, for what we are doing, you need absolute faith. Total belief."

"Belief in what?"

"In the success of *our* future." As she says this she cups her hand as if holding a heavy globe. "Our mistakes of the past have forced us to act. But," she shakes her head, clearing her throat, pulling her chair forward so her breasts lie just over the table, "you are stuck holding on to your friends, just as they're stuck on keeping alive a way of life that simply isn't possible anymore. You," she pauses, gathering the appropriate venom. "You are the monkeys howling in the trees, and we're standing upright, sharpening our spears. You all squabble over what little we have left and waste even more in the process. Your collective ignorance is astounding."

"Made the cut for what? Standing in a factory line? Torturing people? Running security for you? For—"

"For the Apeiron project." I blink. She waits, another

anchor swaying in my tides of disbelief. "Not everything you hear is a rumor. We're living in a graveyard, a massive accumulation of death, and there's only one way out," she says, holding up an index finger.

"Tell me," I ask. She looks at me and laces her fingers and holds her hands in front of her mouth, eyebrows cocked. "Are you actually launching ships?"

"In the past two years, we've launched seventeen. Two catastrophic failures. We have another launch next week, actually." She speaks with a finality that can only be true.

"How many have landed?"

"We have one colony past the six month threshold, that's Miletus, the one you've heard rumors about. New Athens is three months and thriving, and another approaching six weeks, Gaia." I stare at her face but see nothing.

The pools of blood that have seeped into all of my memories lose their color and the blood on my thighs is cold and dry. Every muzzle flash is mute and spreads no light. Mornings in the bakery smell of ash. The sycamore tree is barren and full of rot. Everything we fought for was a paltry off-key whimper in the grand symphony of hope being conducted despite us. We ignored those with the vision as we devoured ourselves. My breathing is deep and slow.

The contempt in her voice seeps out like pus from an aging wound. "You're all rats, scurrying about in a burning house, biting each other for stale crumbs as the foundation cracks and the roof caves in. We stopped trying to put the flames out long ago, because the flames have consumed most everything worth saving. We've been trying to get the smartest, the strongest, the most hopeful, out of the house. And what do you and your people do aside from eat each other alive? Trip us, hoping we stumble and fall so the fire consumes us all. What you see as a noble and necessary fight is a selfish and shortsighted orgy of the most basic instincts of our species."

"We can still help, there's still time left for us to—"

"Your obsession with yourself, your old ways and your

friends is why you can never be a part of this future. You are weak."

My fear is gone, and she is right. The only thing that remains is a hollowness, a void of missed opportunities, half finished sentences, the spreading fungus of despair feeding on the knowledge that I was fighting for the wrong side my entire life. I tilt my head and lick my lips with a dry tongue. "Will we make it?"

"What do you think?" She looks behind me and nods once. *Of course this how it happens.* I feel a slight pressure in the back of my head and everything goes blank.

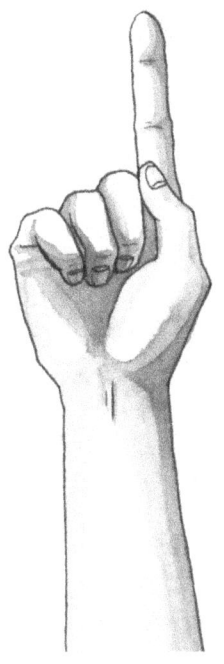

Even Stars Die

Galaxies collide and are lost, scattered forever.

With the infinity that stretches
before and after us
an obsession with the present
seems reasonable.

Lips collide, minds are lost, scattered forever.
Paralysis about the past
and anxiety about what yet's to come
are so common
they've become reasonable.

Even stars die.
And so will you.

The same paths lead only
to the same place.
So go
and get lost.

To enlighten while entertaining. That's my motto. The intersections of technology, the environment, and the unpredictability of being human are what drive my writing.

You are what you eat and what you read.

Choose wisely.